INTERACTIONS

INTERACTIONS

ALEX SOTTO

Interactions

This book is written to provide information and motivation to readers. Its purpose is not to render any type of psychological, legal, or professional advice of any kind. The content is the sole opinion and expression of the author, and not necessarily that of the publisher.

Printed in the United States of America.

ISBN   978-1-951913-13-7   (Paperback)
ISBN   978-1-951913-14-4   (Digital)

Lettra Press books may be ordered through booksellers or by contacting:

Lettra Press LLC
30 N Gould St. Suite 4753
Sheridan, WY 82801, USA
1 303-586-1431 | info@lettrapress.com
www.lettrapress.com

A huge family lived in a big, dilapidated house which incurred a lot of expenses but due to a considerable inheritance, they were able to afford it. The father wasn`t usually around since he lived in the farm down south. Only the mother was present who could not instill discipline and obedience due to her feminine form. The house was situated in a posh residential area and the neighbors all had a fleet of cars at their disposal. The village was surrounded with high walls which shielded it from the noise of the traffic.

On a hot summer`s day you could hear the sparrows chirping melodiously from the treetops. It would rain really hard during the wet season when the typhoon with all its fury would knock down power lines and tree saplings. The monsoon rains were typical of the tropical climate to which this story is set. But during the time of Lent, the vegetation would wither due to a lack of rain.

The clothing that the people wore in this part of the world was flimsy and light. You could sleep soundly in the park with not a layer of clothing and still feel the warmth of the sun.

That is why perhaps the poor are happy here because they don`t have to worry about sub-zero temperatures. It is summer all year round and you see a wide variety of birds that come nesting in these tropical shores. From shorebirds to cattle egrets and blue billed kingfishers, the beauty of nature is at it`s peak. Nevertheless, you had to go to the countryside to experience these things and to see firsthand the symbiotic relationship between the animals.

But there they were, cooped up in a house getting on each other`s nerves. A little faux pas or slip of the tongue would provoke a tumultuous reaction that it would shake the house to its foundation.

There were better days when the family lived harmoniously until one brother got steeped in alcohol, another went into drugs and yet another smoked like a chimney. Of all of them, one brother was a vain person who took to abstract painting following the style of the famous Rothko. That's because he couldn't quite paint the limbs and body parts accurately so he put his efforts on the blending of colors. One brother commented that his painting looked like pigeon droppings and yet another brother, the one who smoked, had the audacity to remove the painting from the living room which started a fight. A very dysfunctional famjily with each member showing the strength of his or her own free will.

Let me start with the brother who paints. He had a native name but anglicized it to make it sound more American. Such was the trend of the times when local performers would belt out tunes from American singers. Colonial mentality was so prevalent in the country that even their given names were of American coinage. Only their last names retained their Spanish heritage which was handed down from one generation to the next. He was called Jack and was born under the sign of Gemini. He had a dual personality much like that of Dr. Jekykll and Mr. Hyde. He had a miniature pinscher with whom he was gentle with and pampered him with canned pet food he bought from the supermarkets. But woe to him who crossed his path. He could unleash so much fury that the hair on your back would stand on end.

He fought relentlessly and never gave his opponent room to breath. He would mouth invectives out of the blue and shatter the stillness of the evening with his loud, sharp-edged voice. If you were the target of his insults, there was no way you could get a good night's sleep. He would slam the door of his room so hard that you could hear it from far away. The only way to remedy the situation is to kill him but the residents being effeminate were not capable of stabbing Jack on the throat or firing bullets from a pîstol. Besides, there was no gun in the house, just a bunch of frayed nerves.

Jonas, the brother who smoked, bore the brunt of Jack's wrath. It all started when Jonas kept the TV set in the closet to deprive Jack and a sister their viewing pleasure. Jack summoned Jonas to a fight downstairs and everything went upside down. They were all over each other, punching and kicking until Jonas'ear turned black. Jonas was clearly overwhelmed by Jack due to his lighter weight. Some other members of the family heard the commotion and broke up the fight.

The days that followed were not at all pleasant. Jonas, who was weaker of the two, no longer ate at the family table and instead had the food brought upstairs. It was never the same again for the peace had already been shattered and Jack persisted in harassing Jonas any which way he can. Jack wrote letters to their eldest sister putting the character of Jonas in a bad light. The main motive of Jack`s war path was to kick Jonas out of the house. He said so himself when he was down by the pool giving the dogs a bath. But there was no way Jonas would leave the house because he had nowhere else to go. Besides, Jonas hadn`t given up his rights to the house which was the property of their mother.

Due to the deterioration of his condition, Jonas was sent to a psychologist for an assessment. He told the psychologist of a harrowing experience, one which continued to this day. Jonas had said that it was difficult to resolve this crisis because the attacks were constant and unrelenting. The psychologist told Jonas to refrain from listening to opera because this would put the spirit in a somber mood. Most of the time, Jonas was nervous and uptight and the visits to a psychologist didn`t help to allay his torment. It was only when Jack went to work and was temporarily out of the house that Jonas could heave a sigh of relief. If there was anything to describe hell, it was living with his brother.

Although they were brothers, Jonas and Jack were worlds apart. You wouldn`t guess they were brothers. Jonas was fair-skinned with a tall nose while Jack was dark with a flat nose. Jonas took after the physical attributes of his father who was a mestizo. Their father had a strong Spanish background and spoke Spanish to his mother. Jonas`father enrolled him in an international school where he learned Spanish from native speakers. He excelled in his classes and got good grades. Soon he put his Spanish to practice and began reading novels from Spanish authors. It was because of his proficiency in Spanish that he later got a scholarship to study in Spain. It was a wonderful experience mingling with the Spaniards and eating Spanish cuisine everyday. He would dip churros, a Spanish pastry, on a hot cup of thick chocolate or delight in a generous serving of paella.

He interacted with the Spaniards and often conversed with people on the street. His vocabulary of the Spanish language had improved. He was intrigued by the dark-skinned gypsies who would sing and play instruments while begging for alms. The gysies were incorporated in the novels of Spanish writers who wrote favorably of them. They contribute a lot to the rich fabric of Spanish culture.

The stores were well stocked with souvenirs, trinkets and other memorabilia. He bought a belt with a buckle that showed a crest of Spanish aristocracy. Since Jonas had a Spanish ancestor, he wondered if he could trace his lineage by doing research on the origin of names. He wondered whether his ancestor had a family crest like most Spanish families.

Walking along a broad boulevard he encountered a blond whore who ushered him into a room. It was the first tine he had sex with a woman. Jonas was intoxicated at the time and lying in bed he saw the whore going through his pants which were hung on the wall. The whore wanted more money to pay for the sexual gratification that she gave.

Is it true what people say that the female genitalia is like a slot machine offered to the highest bidder? When you go out with a woman be prepared to dole out big sums of money to satisfy her craving. It was Eve after all who gave the fruit to Adam. A woman has many demands. She needs a house, a car and a whole assortment of appliances to make her life easier. She is the one who manages the household. The one who will raise the children. The one who keeps the keys of the house. And the one who holds the purse with hundred dollar bills in it. If you can`t provide the basic necessities to a woman, then I suggest you put off any notion of marriage. In case of a break-up, she can always drag you to court and sue you for alimony. Don`t get serious with a woman unless you want to get flayed by her insatiable appetite for material wealth. How is it that the man brings home the bacon and the woman just lolls about and spreads her legs?

I have heard women talk dirty and express their desire for a big cock. They`re like an empty hole waiting to be filled. You should have seen the disappointment on the girl`s face when by the contours in my pants she saw a slightly less size than she had imagined. But being good in bed is no guarantee that you`ll keep you spouse. As time passes, your wife will yearn for a new partner, a fresh face. I have heard of wealthy women have solicited the services of a gigolo. They're tired of the old prune and want some adventure. At an age when they have everything they want except a young hunk who is good in bed. But this is a fleeting fancy. As soon as they get tired of their lover, they go back to their husbands' side to reassert their claim on the conjugal properties. Nothing satisfies their lust more than those diamond rings on their fingers or those expensive brooches on their lapels.

Another marriage that was shaky was that of my brother, Francisco. He was a tall, lean guy who could very well be an excellent basketball player. His hands could touch the net and shoot the ball easily with one small step. He married this woman who came from the hinterlands. Some of his sisters were opposed to the marriage saying she was of a poor background. Nevertheless, she was the only one who volunteered to marry my brother despite his drinking problem. After bearing him two sons and a few years into the marriage, she left my brother and sought refuge in a separate house. He had no job and didn't have an income. My mother argued that my brother's family had given them a business selling rice. The store was managed by his wife's sister and kept them busy. But the income derived from the store wasn't enough to satisfy the needs of the growing household. A few years after my mother died, we all got to inherit a considerable sum of money. After my brother took hold of his share of the inheritance, he was able to lure back his wife and obviously came back. Now they are happy with two adult children who have jobs in the city. Money talks and as long as there is wealth, then the woman will stay. I know of many situations whose wives left their husbands because of financial problems. They reclaimed their single states just so they can look for a man with a better means of support. It is the second nature of a woman to look for a good provider even if it means marrying again. I'm not saying that men shouldn't get married. I'm just saying it's an uphill battle just to keep the marriage intact. Even in a Catholic country where wives make the vow at the altar to stick with their husbands in sickness and in health, for richer or poorer, for better or for worse, they hardly abide by their promise and run off to look for men with money.

Their mother was a kind, caring woman. They had a big table with many chairs where everyone ate lunch and dinner. One time she wrote a letter to her husband saying she felt like that old woman who lived in a shoe. She should have practiced family planning so she could attend to the needs of her children more attentively. Instead, she left them to the care of nannies and sent them to school in chauffeur driven cars. She had fourteen children in all, seven boys and seven girls. Her favorite past time was playing mahjong with other rich women of her age. She was born before the war and escaped the grip of the enemy soldiers by going to one island to another in a boat. Others weren`t as lucky. Some women served as comfort woman acting as sex slaves to the soldiers in uniform. They never expected to be invaded by a foreign power and had to elude capture by all means conceivable. Her older brother was killed by the invaders and left a void that was difficult to fill.

She had a brother, Hector, who was a radio operator during the war. He was awarded with U.S. citizenship after the war and moved to that northern country subsequently. He later died leaving a vast fortune to his siblings.

Our mother married our father after the war. He was impressed by the many properties our mother`s family owned. She was of the indigenous ancestry but could still speak Spanish as this was the language at that time. She moved her family to the capital city but still spoke the vernacular at home. You sound sweet speaking this language even though you are angry.

She had the cook prepare her a soup every morning with leafy vegetables and small silvery fishes with white meat. She didn`t have exquisite tastes. She was a native down to the core. Her choice of husband, however, revealed her preference for caucasians. Her small stature stood opposite to that of her tall husband. Her husband looked like Rock Hudson while you could mistake her for a maid.

Our mother had a religious upbringing and later in life would go to church everyday. She always told Jonas not to miss out on Sunday mass but these words fell on deaf ears. Seeking a livelihood meant a full time job and he practically had no time to fulfill his devoctions. But Jonas read books about his Catholic faith and never really abandoned his religion.

On the other hand, her husband didn`t go to church. He drew his wisdom from books of famous writers. He was also a philanderer who chased skirts even in the farm. In one letter he wrote to our mother, he bragged about the numerous affairs with different sorts of ladies. Becauseof his dashing good looks, he was able to bait blondes, brunettes and redheads. But our mother took it with a grain of salt saying he was an incurable playboy. Instead of expanding the family business, he spent his time cavorting with all kinds of women including househelp and ladies from remote areas. He regretted not purchasing land in a popular island resort. He wasn`t a savvy investor and had a deficient business sense. Instead, he lend cash to farmers in exchange for sacks of rice. At the end of the day, he filled his barns with many bags of grain that he would later mill and sell as white rice ready for consumption. The business survives until this day with my brother`s family at the helm of operations. My father urged his children to do physical exercise and encouraged our mother to quit smoking. He said that it was hard to give up the habit in the first few days but that the only way to quit was cold turkey. But our mother continued to smoke even in her old age. Our cousins didn`t have a highregard for our father. One cousin called him a loan shark. But that simply wasn`t the case. Sacks of rice could be stacked in a barn without growing old. It was like going back to the barter trade. Farmers could turn in their produce instead of paying their loans in cash. Rice was a staple food of the people and didn`t rot as long as it was stored in a dry place.

Meanwhile in Spain, all was not well with Jonas. It was true he was receiving a stipend from the Spanish government but he had to pay rent to the landlady who came from the same country as he did. And besides, he had a roommate who complained about his snoring. Jonas was kicked out of the room and had to sleep in the study which was filled with books. His roommate`s name was Gerard who was a very clean guy. He liked to think of himself as a girl and grew his hair to his shoulders. They both went to the same university and studied a special six month course for scholars. Gerard would wear make-up to school and it made our classmates wonder whether it was all a game. Later, through the insistence of Gerard, Jonas moved out of the house of their landlady and lodged in a hostel which was an affordable public housing ideal for travellers. At the end of the course, Jonas was awarded with two diplomas. One diploma was for the entirety of the course and the other was for the thesis he did for a professor. Gerard worked as an English teacher and underwent taunts from his fellow teachers because of his overtly feminine manners and dress. But he succeeded in his job and stayed in Spain for a long time. Jonas didn't have any experience working nor did he have the foresight of things to come. He had no job and no savings which only meant that he wouldn't be able to survive in Spain. Jonas was also suffering from mental afflictions. Days before he left for Spain, a brother who was close to him attempted to commit suicide. No matter how much he pleaded with his mother to pass the phone to his brother, the mother refused his request. Jonas began doubting about the health of his favorite brother. His name was Manuel of whom I shall be talking about later.

Needless to say, the scholarship which covered the period of one year was running out. And Jonas still hadn't found an alternative source of income. Right now Jonas was staying in the home of another compatriot who had two small children. She offered Jonas the chance to work in a job site as they had a contact there. But Jonas did not respond to the offer and opted instead to go back to his country of origin. So the husband of the woman brought Jonas to the airport and boarded a plane bound for the far east. There was no way Jonas could work things out in Spain as he was in agony. A classmate of his counselled him to go back home because he was a nervous wreck. And so he did and gave up the dream of living in Europe. It wasn't long when Jonas was back in the house where he grew up. His sister Cecille remarked that he lost his chance to liven in Europe. Life in the far east was that of grinding poverty and a lot of people would do anything to be given a chance to live in Europe. There was a big difference between the life in the far east and Europe. In Europe there were hardly any beggars in the street while in the far east the inhabitants lived in slums. Many times there is no running water and sanitation. Street urchins and blind folks led by their guides would beg from passengers of parked cars. Under the blistering sun they would spend the whole day begging for money. On sidewalks and churches you see them too lying on straw mats with their arms outstretched asking for mercy. But the passersby walk by passively so used to seeing such misery. Many slum dwellers would fall ill due to the toxic fumes they breathe. Some TV programs feature the desperate state of poor people who ask for donations so they can get medical treatment. Hospital stays and medical intervention can be costly because there is no government insurance to cover the expenses.

The problem with this country is it has a high birthrate. Artificial contraception is frowned upon and abortion is illegal. Native women of child bearing age don`t stop having children until they have given birth to a great number of infants. The runaway population growth is depletingthe resources of the country. The Catholic church, which exerts a strong influence on the government and the people, can be blamed on the high birthrate because of its stern opposition to birth control. Unlike the U.S. which enshrined the separation of church and state in its constitution, the church has the power to terminate the services of a government official because of moral turpitude. Take for instance the Movie and TV review board. Two of its chairmen were fired for allowing movies with explicit sex scenes to be shown in theaters. Meanwhile because of poverty, underage children are plying the sex trade in exchange for money. Why do mothers bring so many children into this world if they can`t take care of them? Many times it is the parent who sells his daughter to big time spenders. Often times their daughters run away from home and find themselves in a worse predicament. They`re often in the hands of pimps who make them work in beer gardens and nightclubs in the red light district. Tourists from all over the world come here so they can spend the night with some cheap prostitute.

The government lacks the financial capacity to educate the young girls so they can have an alternative source of livelihood. Many girls are illiterate not knowing how to read or write. Girls in the hinterlands spend the whole day in the rice fields or make the water buffalo graze through the dry grass. They are lured into the city by unscrupoulous men who promise them a better life. Instead of finding a decent job, the girls work in unventilated factories or end up as prostitutes. They were better off where they came from.

One way to alleviate poverty is to improve the status of women. The government should invest money on the improvement of education making it free and compulsory to young men and women. Only by honing their langage skills and helping them acquire training will we finally see an eradication of poverty.

Many countries in Europe and North America have already gotten rid of poverty raising the standard of living to an optimum level. Here every citizen has access to quality education, medical insurance and social services that are denied in poorer countries. That is why there are a lot of illegal immigrants who are trying to enter the country so they can escape poverty and unemployment. In this part of the world, the majority of the population are employed as domestic helpers. The only way to drastically improve the situation is to move to a wealthier country.

In this part of the world, corruption is rampant. Swindlers are hardly prosecuted because they give kickbacks to government officials. The executive branch which includes the president is the arm of government that steals with impunity. Even the wife of a dictator who stole millions of dollars never spent a day in jail. Her assets abroad were seized but she is as free as a bird.

During the hispanic era, the church and the state were one and the same. So much power was vested in the Spanish friar that they ruled the islands with an iron fist. They ruled the country for 300 years and left their mark everywhere. They built churches, universities, hospitals andeven a walled city called Intramuros. One example of a church they built was the San Agustin church which is situated in Intramuros. It is an imposing structure with thick walls, angels carved stone, and an immense dome. It has withstood the test of time because even with the frequent passage of typhoons and earthquakes, the church stands majestic to this day. The Spanish friar introduced the Catholic faith to the natives and gave them Spanish surnames like Mendoza, Castillo and de la Cruz to name a few.

They also built the University of Santo Tomas which is older than Harvard university. Courses on medicine and law are offered here. They also erected Letran which is a school of the elite.

The culmination of Spanish architecture was the construction of Intramuros. The streets are paved with cobble stones and trees line the streets. You can go for a ride in a horse drawn buggy and pass a wide variety of shops and commerce. The residence of the governor general is situated in this walled city. But through it all, the Spanish friar had a lot of influence on the daily lives of the people. They owned vast tracts of land where workers toiled everyday so that crops could grow and trees bear fruit. They owned sugarcane plantations and consolidated their holdings even in the coastal areas of the muslim south. They ran the sugar mills and instructed the women how to weave the pineapple fabric. They paid the workers their daily wage and since there was no inflation, one peso could buy you a bag of groceries. One friar even studied an indigenous language and compiled a highly comprehensive dictionary. It is a valuable piece of writing that is still being used by scholars.

But there was a dark side to the Spanish friar. Some of them broke their vow of chastity, which is a prerequisite for entering the religious life, and impregnated the local women. It is the subject of a book by a native writer who wrote about the excesses of the friar. A lot of native men went to study in Spain and tried to petition the government there toleave the country. They were being ruled by a foreign power who gave them no representation in the Spanish congress. By the nineteenth century, the fight for independence had begun.

One day Jonas met a distant cousin of his who told him that one of his ancestors was a Spanish friar. This piece of news gave him chills down his spine. His cousin's name was Rafael who had strong European features. He also told Jonas that another ancestor was born in Spain. He showed Jonas the birth certificate of this great great grandfather that will attest to the fact that he was a Spaniard. It was a meeting that was well worth it because through Rafael, Jonas was informed of his origins. Rafael was a painter who did portraits of angels. He was a highly skilled artist and sold a lot of his works in art galleries.

Unfortunately, Jonas went back to his country of origin only to be harassed by his brother, Jack. The fighting escalated and Jonas sought refuge in the farm. Here he found peace and enjoyed the company of his father. His father berated Francisco who didn't stop drinking. The ongoing conflict became more and more violent because Francisco didn't want to give up the bottle. Even the psychiatrist confided to our mother that is was very hard to cure an alcoholic. Only the invisible force from up above can help cure a drunkard.

Francisco had a very low self-esteem. His aunt gave him a huge sum of money which he squandered. Many times he would come home drunk after a day of carousing with his buddies. He lost his watch after it came off from his hand in the sandy road. After he married, he finally found a wife who would cook for him and take care of him. He mentioned that he should have gotten married earlier which would have been a catastrophe given his penchant for drinking and poor financial status. Who knows what will happen when he runs out of money. The wife might run away and leave him all by his lonesome self. Only time will tell.

Eventually, Jonas went back to live in the house of his mother. He met a Spanish teacher who trained him how to teach Spanish grammar. Jonas grew adept at this job and had a commanding stage presence. He was after all talking in front of many students. He taught his students to think methodically and some who paid close attention to the instruction, turned out to be proficient writers in the language.

The friend of Jonas, William Gomez, ran a weekly newspaper. Jonas contributed articles to the paper and was well received by his colleagues. William was gay and had a lover living in his house. Because of this, there were some gentlemen who were not in favor of him joining the Academy. Nevertheless, because of his exceptional talent at writing and fluency in the Spanish language, he was named a member of the Academy. William said that having sex was like drinking water. It is so commonplace that most everyone does it. As long as the sex was consensual and between two adults, then one should have no difficulty in achieving your goals. No law was brokien.

William was a leading figure in the defense and promotion of the Spanish language in the country. The Spanish embassy conferred him an honroary title and called him the champion defender of the Spanish language. He was invited to all of the functions and fiestas of the embassy. He blamed the Americans for the erosion of the Spanish language and culture. The Americans came in the beginning of the twentieth century after defeating the Spaniards. They forced everyone to learn the English language and thus the natives lost their hispanic identity. William wrote scathing articles and books about the imposition of the English language by the White Anglo-Saxon Protestants. He argued that the only way to understand the history of the native culture is through the knowledge of Spanish. That`s because most of the literature and history books were written in Spanish.

William was a man of many talents. Aside from writing, he also taught flamenco. A bevy of beauties surround him whenever there is an event. The girls wear flowers in their hair, flowing dresses with ruffles, and shoes that make a quick succession of loud tapping noises on the floor. They complete their regalia with castanets on their hands which make a lively clicking sound when hit against the palm of the hand. The dancers rehearsed everyday and executed synchronized movements.

Although William was a homosexual, his parents forced him to get married because he was an only child. They wanted him to produce offspring so they could pass down their name to the next generation. William had two children, a son and a daughter. The daughter died of brain cancer and left some children behind. While she was alive, she was a talented flamenco dancer. There are many pictures of her wearing flamenco costume and finery. Her father was a recipient of a prestigious literary prize. She left behind a widower who was a wealthy man from the south.

In one of William`s lectures he explained because of the coming of the Spaniards, the spread of Islam was stopped. Had it not been for the establishment of Catholicism, Islam would have been propagated in the whole archipelago. Catholicism is a more lenient religion that gives women the freedom to wear what she chooses. Unlike the muslim women who have to cover their faces with a veil.

The women in Islamic countries are like second class citizens because they can`t even go out of their homes without a male escort. They have no right to divorce their husband and can`t even own a driver`s license. The Spanish regime put the woman on an equal footing with their male counterpart. The woman is this country is no oppressed nor is she relegated to the sidelines. She is front and center in the affairs of the state even having elected two female presidents. But because of the onerous practices of the Catholic church that forbid the use of artificial contraception, the woman is burdened with having to care for many children.

A profound understanding developed between William and Jonas.

William treated Jonas to lunches at Spanish restaurants and, in return, Jonas would be a substitute teacher for classes whenever William had an engagement and had to be absent. It wasn`t hard to teach the class because there was a textbook that guided Jonas how to teach the lesson of the day. They went on for years until William reached retirement age. When William left the university, he received a hefty retirement pay. The friendship lasted for along time until the lover of William started getting jealous. His name was Roger Sison and was picked up at a club where he was doing dirty dancing. But because of his impressive physique, he placated the erotic fantasies of William. He massaged William with lotion, powder and aromatic oils. He would play a sexy song on the turntable and do a private striptease. All this he did before William went to bed and slept soundly with sweet dreams. Sometimes when William had trouble sleeping, they would go to a bar to rub elbows with other single bachelors and invite men for an orgy in a motel. William had time for some nocturnal adventures because he was already retired. He was old but still craved for some handsome company. Roger cast an icy look on Jonas who he deemed as his competitor. In one of their frank conversations Roger told William to stop seeing Jonas. He told William it was either him alone or he would leave him. William pleaded with him to stop bickering saying that he was just reorienting Jonas so he could be exposed to Spanish culture.

Since William›s retirement from the university, the role of Jonas in William›s life was greatly diminished. Jonas was however invited whenever there was a show of flamenco dancers. The presence of Jonas in the house agitated Roger. Roger planned to do something that would shake the neighborhood.

One night when William came home from some dancing, kissed and hugged by several of his dancers as he bade them goodbye, he was greeted by Roger Sison who stood by the doorway.

William was surprised by his rough demeanor and said Waited for me for a long time?

Roger was visibly irked by his tardiness and said, The night is young. We have the whole night to chat. I hope you don't have any engagements tomorrow cause I plan to stay up the whole night with you.

William tried to soothe his anxiety, I have no rehearsals tomorrow. The girls need some rest from their hectic schedule.

Roger led the way upstairs to the bedroom and turned on the chandelier. William purchased the chandelier from a furniture store situated on a busy thoroughfare. He specifically chose it for the crystal ornaments that hung from the spokes. It was the artistic side of William that shone from his choice of furniture. Even the bed with it's four posts were made of oak and the drawers were made from hardwood mahogany. They sat on the chairs at the little corner of the room.

With a sullen look Roger said, «I told you that I didn›t want you hanging around with Jonas. I don›t care if he›s your assistant but you seem to be giving him too much attention.»

William tried to calm him down, «I›ve known Jonas for many years and all I›m doing is reorienting him to Spanish culture.» William swallowed. «There is no reason why you should be preoccupied. Jonas is a harmless young man and I value his friendship because he contributes articles to my newspaper.»

But Roger could not contain his emotions, «How do I know you›re not being intimate with Jonas? The way you both laugh and the free lunches he gets from you? For all you know he might be lying in the same bed with you."

William tried to reassure Roger, «My friendship with jonas is merely platonic. He shows an interest in what I do and the door is always open to admirers and beginners. It's my way of disseminating Spanish culture in the country. I can't just perform for a handful of people. The message should be spread to the public at large."

But Roger couldn›t hide his feelings. «I can›t help but feel jealous everytime Jonas is here."

William tried to convince Roger that he was the only one he shared his bed with. He came after sundown when everyone had already retired to their chambers. No one has seen him except perhaps the cleaning woman who left the house rather late in the day. He couldn›t possibly put a picture frame of Roger in the middle of the room because he wanted the world to know that he was clean inside and out. His tryst with Roger was better kept a secret, hidden from view.

William was feeling hot and queasy wearing his flamenco costume and wanted to slip into something more comfortable. Roger assisted him undressing down to his leather boots and helped him put on satin pajamas. They both had a can of beer to ease their frayed nerves. After a night of dancing, it was necessary to relax and stretch with some alcohol.

There was a knock on the door. It was Elsa the cleaning lady who wanted to notify William that she was going home after a hard days work.

«Did some overtime?» asked Roger. But Elsa disregarded him preferring instead to fix her attention on William. «I placed a thermos with hot water on your night table and put your towels on a rack in the bathroom. Is there anything else I can do for you?» inquired Elsa. «We›re quite okay here, thank you. I don›t know what I'd do without you Elsa. You can go." replied William.

Roger gave Elsa that icy look as if he was warning her to be careful. Elsa stared back at Roger nonplussed but considering it was late at night, quickly sped off and went downstairs. Now William and Roger were all alone in the house. The warm air seeped through the windows and it as pitch dark outside. All you could see were the street lamps illuminating the street and occassionally a car would pass by. It was a cloudless night and the silvery moon was full and bright.

Roger wanted to probe the consciousness of William. He wanted to know where he stood and if William had a place for him in his life. With raised eyebrows he asked «Are you ashamed of me? Why don›t you introduce me to your fiends? Give me a seat in your shows instead of just visiting you almost every night."

This question caught William off guard and he responded « No one must know what we›re doing. No one must know that I have a lover. Be thankful I even picked you up from that sleazy strip joint where you perform doing all those lewd dances. You won›t sit well with the academe. With me you have a roof over your head just as long as you let me do my daily activities. But you have to do something about your possessiveness. There›s no reason for you to be jealous with the people I hang around with.» There was a pause, a brief lull in their discussion. William took a tea bag and poured some hot water in a cup. He took a sip and with a renewed interest faced Roger. "So what have you planned for tonight?"

Roger had an idea and suggested «We can go to a bar and drink some hard liquor. Later we can pick up a guy and have a threesome. No one will recognize you, if that is what you›re worried about. The place is dimly lit and the cover of darkness will protect your identity.»

But William declined and said «I›m already in my pajamas and I›m tired after so much flamenco dancing. Maybe we could be together in bed. Just the two of us with not a soul watching us.» William blushed a little as he said this but he knew he wanted some male company. He wanted to caress masculine arms and slide his fingers on bulging muscles and gently kiss the hairy chest of a well-built hunk. It was the very nature of William to hug an Adonis and play games during the night.

Roger fit the description of a well-hung guy, a gigolo who made lonely people happy. He was reared from a broken home with his parents separating at an early age. He never really got a good education and can hardly read or write. But inspite of the dismal circumstances that surrounded his childhood, he grew up to be a healthy lad with sufficient looks and considerable height.

Roger explained his situation «I have a problem making ends meet. The cost of living has gone way up and what I earn from the strip joint can't cover my expenses. Even with the tips, I don't earn enough to pay for my room and board. I was wondering perhaps if I can move in here permanently."

William tried to resolve the issue by saying «I have a parcel of land down south which I inherited from a rich uncle. Maybe I can put you there. You›ll be among the geese, the chickens and the goats which isn›t a bad idea. My caretaker will show you how everything works. You will have a meager consumption of electricity. Just a bed and a hole on the floor that will serve as a toilet. It›s back to basics. The life in the farm is simple. You will find everything you need in that plot of land. You can even grow tomatoes, cucumber and fruit trees. This is a token of my appreciation for all the services you rendered. Meanwhile, hang in there. I still need your company to spice up my nights a little."

But Roger voiced a little apprenhension «I don't know whether the rustic life in the farm will suit me. I was raised in the city and had gotten used to the noise of the traffic. Why don't you just let me live in this house. If you can entertain Jonas, surely you can give in to my petition."

They were in disagreement. William knew he had to give something to help defray the costs of Roger›s standard of living. But considering there was limited space in the house, William replied «I can›t have you here during the day. My students come and go and soon they›ll be wondering who you are. I know you play a vital role in my life because you give me pleasure and satisfy my urges. But that›s all I can offer you. My resources are limited and if that doesn›t suit you then we might as well call it quits.»

Roger relented albeit begrudgingly and accepted the offer of William. At the rate he was going, Roger would›ve accepted anything because he was in an exceedingly dire situation. He was scrounging for money in the dance floor and relied on tips from patrons to eke out a living. The sex trade was the only kind of livelihood he knew. Without training and no university education, his chances of getting a good job were close to nil. And besides due to the poor performance of the country's financial sector, employment opportunities were few and far between. He'd have to look for a rich person to supply his needs. And William's status in life had to be enough for now. He was like a leech that sucked the life out of William.

William offered Roger a plate of coffee cream pie. Roger had a ravenous appetite not having eaten the whole afternoon. He licked the plate clean including the crust and asked for another serving. Roger lived in the slums and would welcome anything to improve his lot in life.

Then William made him a propostion «Have you ever had sex with a woman? Maybe fallen in love with a girl?"

Roger wondered what William was up to and didn›t deny that he was a promiscuous person and had intercourse with all kinds of people. The customers at the strip joint were both male and female, lonely matrons and rich gay men who were in search of some nocturnal adventure. Well yes, Roger had had relations with the opposite sex.

William then wryly suggested that he look for a rich widow to support him as a last ditch effort to save his skin. But Roger stated that he had found his gold mine and that was to be in the loving arms of William. Just the two of them with no interference from outside forces.

Roger then kissed William on both cheeks and shook his hand. But William pursed his lips and wanted more. He wanted a torrid kiss with tongues in each other›s mouth. What followed was a scene of intense sensuality. They both lied in bed smacking each other on the lips. But this was a just a foretaste of things to come. The night was still young and the darkness served as an ideal backdrop for a romantic interlude.

Out of the blue, William raised the picture frame of his daughter and showed it to the four corners of the room. With a heavy heart he launched into a heartfelt soliloquy about the unexpected loss of his daughter.

"Oh my daughter, my heart aches due to your sudden departure. It was as if someone tore you from my life. How can I ever recover from your absence? You are no longer at my side, unable to hear the thunderous applause, the adulation from your cheering fans after we executed our flawless dance number. You looked ravishing in your flamenco outfit which suited you well with your Spanish heritage. Your effortless grace became even more pronounced with every step of your bright red shoes. So many men fell in love with your hispanic features as they tried to woo you to become their muse. You were the subject of many painters as they tried to capture the enigmatic smile of your rare beauty. You stood out among your peers delivering a commanding stage presence on every venue you danced. Alas, you left us too early to give a fitting farewell to an example of good taste and breeding such as you. I always taught you to be proud of your hispanic heritage as Spanish blood courses through your veins. Your fair skin gave a lasting impression of the cultural cross section of our country. The passage of time cannot efface your memory as you leave lasting legacy in the art of the dance. Nothing can tarnish your reputation as an inspiration to painters and other creatuve geniuses with an artistic expression. Sleep well my dear daughter as we constantly climb the mountain to reach the summit of perfection. With your imperishable flame we will surely attain the peak of performance where your talents have no equal."

With that William kissed and gently laid down the picture frame on his night table as if she were a goddess to be revered and admired. William rummaged through the drawers and brought out a pair of red shoes, the ones his duaghter used to wear. He started to swear "If it weren't for that malignant cancer, my duaghter would still be alive today. Must be my side of the family. We have a predisposition to serious illnesses like cancer, stroke and heat disease. So I thank my lucky stars that I'm still strong and feisty enough to dance. Usually people my age are bound to a wheelchair and unable to walk. Pray that I am in good health because what is good for me is good for you."

Roger›s face was serene at this point and later added his share of life›s ups and downs, «Your duagther was fortunate enough to have experienced the love a father like you. For my part, I never had a family who could support me through trials and great affliction. I was shuttled back and forth from house to house like some sort of merchandise never really able to plant my feet firmly on the ground. My time at Boys Town, a refuge for underage boys, was very trying as I had to share a small space with a horde of other minors. We were woken up at three in the morning to verify if we were safely tucked into bed. They sifted through our bags to see if we had secretly pickpocketed from our fellow batchmates or shoplifted from the place itself. There was an aura of suspicion that hung over our heads. The place wasn't very conducive to be a good and obedient lad. Right now I have nothing. Not a house, not a car, not even a family to call my own. I earn my living any which way I can even if it means selling my flesh. I'll take anything you can give me."

There was a tear in William's eye as he listened intently to the tale of want and deprivation. He sympathized with the doleful predicament of his lover and offered to assuage his anxieties. He took out a cheque book and wrote pay to Cash. He wrote the amount of ten thousand pesos which is roughly the equivalent of two hundred dollars. William didn't think he had a bank account and with this kind of cheque, he thought Roger could take out the cash. William handed the cheque to Roger who gladly accepted it. This amount was to get Roger going for at least a month. He was so moved by the story of Roger that he did not doubt the veracity of his lowly origins. It was a friendly gesture that bridged the gap of people belonging to different social strata. He wanted to show affection and appreciation for the people around him.

William set everything aside and eagerly asked, «So what have you planned for tonight?»

Roger replied, «We›ll play a game tonight. Have you ever tried rough sex?»

William responded in earnest, «I›ve never ventured into something like that but am willing to try something new.»

«Here›s a teaser,» as Roger stuck out his penis for William to perform fellatio. William was grinning with contentment and he exclaimed that Roger was so richly endowed physically that he was on the pink of health.

Roger then instructed William to lie down while he tied the hands and feet of William to the bed posts. Roger was about to perform a sadomasochistic ritual as he took out a whip, the one animal trainers use to tame their beasts. Roger began to whip William until red lacerations surfaced on his skin. William demanded that he be untied immediately and be set free from this physical bondage.

Roger tortured William until he was on the verge of despair. Roger began to rant, «You stingy little pipsqueak". You think the money you gave me would be enough to cover my expenses? You're under my grip now and you will be subject to my every whim." Roger played a song on the phonograph and did a turn moving his body sinuously to the voluptuous rhythm. The sound was so loud that it muffled the plaintive cries of William. There were bruises on his wrists as he twisted his hands in an effort to free himself. William regretted the day he gave shelter to Roger and should have known better than to associate with an ungrateful scumbag.

«Get me out of here!» screamed William but his protestations fell into deaf ears as Roger whipped him some more. «I›ll give you anything you want,» cried William as a last recourse to obtain liberty. But Roger flatly refused to untie him and said «It›s too late. You should have known better than to mess around with me. You reneged on your promise that we›d be a couple instead you invited upstarts to your inner circle. If I could make a list of your shortcomings, I could fill up a whole sheet of paper. If I had to enumerate your faults, it would take the whole morning. You›ve tested my patience long enough and now you›ve reached the point of no return. Your end is coming very soon as I will thrust this knife into your flesh.» With a scornful expression on his face

Roger took out a nine inches kitchen knife from the drawer and without further ado plunged the knife on the throat of William.

The deed was done. Roger lifted the needle of the record player and halted the music. There was a ghastly silence. Just the lifeless body of William spread out on the bed. William never had a chance as he was tethered to the bedposts not able to free himself. Roger showed no mercy even as William pleaded for his life. The sun began to rise. A new day was already dawning. The sunshine filtered through the windows and exposed the night›s terrible tragedy. Roger let out a horrible laughter as if it came from the nether world. It reverberated through the walls of the room. «You had it coming to you,» as he wiped the sweat from his forehead that was trickling down to his cheeks.

There was a light breeze that wafted to William›s room. Roger will never feel remorse for what he did. It was too early to tell whether Roger would have any misgivings for the crime he just committed. He would have to play cat and mouse with the authorities as he covered his tracks so they wouldn›t be able to trace him. He was a non-entity who didn›t even have records in the statistics office. His fingerprints didn›t match the database of wanted criminals as he didn't have any previous citation. Record-keeping was so inaccurate in this country that the past convictions didn't tally with the profile of a wanted felon. Roger came from a center for delinquent youth and the schoolmaster did a headcount of the children present. There were no requirements, no proof of age or identity. They just picked up vagrant children from the street and offered them refuge from the harsh reality. Roger wiped the blood from his hands with a face towel that hung in the bathroom. He put on his pants and shirt and took out a lump sum of cash from William's wallet. After that, Roger left the premises leaving a trail of circumstantial evidence.

In the morning the cleaning lady came to do some household chores. She noticed that it was eerily quiet because by this time William would already be reading the newspaper. But no one came to pick up the paper and she thought that her boss must still be sleeping. Nevertheless, she went up the stairs and found the door unlocked. She opened the door and made the gruesome discovery of William›s corpse tied to the bed. The cleaning lady shrieked in horror and went down to call the police.

The news of William's untimely demise was broadcast on the local

TV station. Jonas heard about the grisly murder of his friend and after a few days paid his respects at the church where the coffin lay. It was a sealed casket with his only son receiving sympathizers. He was obviously distraught and laden with sorrow. He was sobbing uncontrollably but managed to greet the visitors. The diplomatic circle was shocked by the turn of events and sent a wreath to adorn the chapel. The Spanish ambassador signed the book of condolences, as well as, other dignitaries. William was well-loved and admired for his contributions to the artistic and literary scene. A shining light on Spanish language and culture in the country has been extinguished. Tributes poured forth from here and abroad as a writer of history and culture has been silenced by this dastardly deed.

William›s homosexuality was a facet few people knew about. His promiscuity spelled disaster for him as he was risking his life to be in the company of people of ill-repute. He was courting danger by sleeping with men who were not in his category. It was a miscalculation that cost him his life.

The president of the republic intervened in the investigation and dispatched the army to help secure the house. The house was cordoned off as police and detectives were busy scouring the place in search of clues that could serve as evidence. They found the bloodied knife on the floor that investigators carefully put in a plastic bag for examination of finger prints in the lab. The weapon they believe was used in the murder. They wanted to interrogate the cleaning lady whose name was Elsa but she was heavily sedated and still in shock confined in a hospital. They waited for a few days until everything calmed down before they could talk to her. They argued she would most likely have met the culprit since she was in the house every day. They examined the ropes used to tie the victim and the bed for any trace of body fluids and human hair that could lead to the identity of the criminal. It was a most heinous crime one that left investigators baffled from the outset. In the first place, there was no sign of forced entry so the suspect must have been known to the victim. And the sexual orientation of the victim was called into question since he was married before and had a regimented daily schedule. Here was a busy man who rose to the top of the academe and hobnobbed with the high society. Why would anyone put a knife on the throat of someone renowned and of great stature? And why would anyone leave him in a bed tied up to a post in a degrading position?

After a few days, the police were able to interview Elsa from her hospital bed. She was dressed in a blue hospital gown with furry slippers. She sat straight as she sipped some juice to clear her throat. Elsa had a vivid recollection of a man who slept at William›s house. Her description matched the identity of Roger although she didn›t know his name. The police were able to sketch a portrait of the assailant. He had black wavy hair that reached his shoulders, medium build with bushy eyebrows and brown complexion. Soon the police made posters that was an accurate depiction of the prime suspect. A hefty reward was offered for information leading to the arrest of the individual. Do not approach the suspect as he is deemed to be armed and dangerous. Just call the police station and relay his whereabouts.

Elsa left the hospital in a wheelchair unable to walk due to the traumatic experience she had discovering the mangled body of her employer. She went home to her apartment and kissed the only picture she had of her boss which was in a picture frame. She wept silently and reminisced of the good times she had working for William.

She laid down on her bed and looked up at the ceiling noticing that cobwebs had accumulated in the corner. She was too tired to pick up the duster and wipe away the particles. The brutal slaying of her master was still ingrained in her mind. She tried to distract the flashbacks that were recurring in her head by reading magazines or watching wholesome films in her videoplayer but to no avail. The bloody scene still sent her shivers and made her hair stand on end. She took tranquilizers to calm her nerves and to help her sleep. She closed her eyes and minutes later she fell into a deep slumber.

She dreamt about her master dressed in a white robe beckoning to her. He didn›t say anything but invited her to come closer. There was a snake around his neck that seemed to strangle him. She tried to engage him in a conversation to see what she could do. But at this point her master was seated in a ferris wheel that brought him up briefly to the clouds and down again. The wheel turned for a few times and the doorbell rang. Her sleep was interrupted and she woke up.

Elsa answered the door with furry slippers and her hair all messed up because she had just woken up and didn't have the time to fix herself up. It was Sister Claire dressed in a nun's habit with her hair and ears covered by a gray hood. She did volunteer work for an outreach program with the Archdiocese of St. Francis visiting seniors and solitary people in their homes to keep them company and talk with them. She brought a box of camomille tea and a box of soca crackers.

«I was sleeping when you came,» said Elsa. «Woke up from a bad dream. Don›t you know what happened? My boss was murdered and I saw firsthand the decaying cadaver on the bed.»

«I know,» replied Sister Claire. «I heard it over the news. You must be feeling tense. I›m here to give you comfort and you can talk to me about your troubles.»

Elsa wiped a tear from her eye and began to recount in gory detail about the dream she had of her master. Sister Claire listened attentively serving the tea and crackers. She warned Elsa that due to the botched circumstances behind his death, her master was trying to tell her something. Deceased people often communicates with us while we›re sleeping appearing to us as ghosts seeking closure to their lives on earth. That means the soul is in a turbulent state while the murder is not solved. Sister Claire worked in the vicinity where Elsa lived covering about a six mile radius from the church.

Camomille tea would help pacify the nerves and reinvigorate the brain. Elsa couldn't dwell in the past but had to compose herself and pull ahead with the times. Sister Claire hugged Elsa and told her everything would would be alright. She suggested that they join a church social, the Legion of Mary to be exact, to ward off evil spirits and rub elbows with other parishioners. It was the least they could do to appease the spirits and ask for a favorable outcome of events. The Legion of Mary had a meeting once a week and today was the appointed time for the meeting.

Elsa still had morbid thoughts and her desire for vengeance was full to capacity. He›ll get caught and he›ll have to spend the rest of his life in a dank, dingy cell. There can be no rest until the suspect is arrested. Elsa recounted to Sister Claire her dreadful ordeal and Sister Claire couldn't believe her ears. Sister Claire's mouth went agape due to the bloody and detailed description of the event. Elsa cried on the shoulder of Sister Claire but she hugged her tightly to give her the determination to move on.

Elsa never had suitors. She had a masculine face and were it not for her long, black hair she could have easily passed off as a man. She had an expression of a bulldog that was not suited to romance. She used coconut oil to make her hair shiny and grow thick like a forest. She never wore make-up and carried a shoulder bag where she kept a roll of toilet paper, a packet of mooncakes and a bottle of water. She was always on the road and sometimes had the urge to eat. But this time she was at home reflecting on the days past.

Elsa had a lot of friends mostly domestic workers who›d come by to share the latest gossip. They would pore over the movie magazines and talk about the rumors surrounding their favorite film stars. This they did during holidays and weekends when they›d be off from work.

Elsa fulfilled her duties and what was expected of her. She really cared for William. Aside from tidying the house, she would prepare his meals adding a lot of protein to his diet and excluding carbohydrates which could worsen his sugar intake. She mixed fruit juices in the blender like oranges, mangoes and papaya. William seemed to relish the succulent concoctions and asked for several servings more. For breakfast she would serve him pancakes topped with butter and maple syrup. William gave her her due. She was handsomely rewarded for a job well done.

Elsa had a few encounters with Roger when she was asked to work late at night to fix the bed and prepare his clothes. William would come home late and needed the assistance of Elsa. Elsa wondered who Roger was, hanging around in the bedroom of her master. Little did she know that William was having an affair with this low life. Roger had an unkempt hair and his clothes stunk that needed some washing. Roger gave Elsa the dagger looks implying his displeasure at her presence. His rugged appearance was clearly etched in her memory.

Noticing that Roger was feeling uneasy, William ordered Elsa to leave the room to which she complied. Roger couldn't forget the time when Elsa didn't want to let him in because her master was not at home. Roger eventually went in when William arrived. Elsa could hardly imagine her master in the company of someone from the streets. He struck her as someone subsisting on crumbs and rejects that would do anything for a roof over his head. But Roger's visits were often and this worried Elsa because she knew something was wrong.

The winds were picking up outside and it was getting cloudy. The branches of trees were swaying and there was little sunlight filtering from above. Elsa told Sister Claire to close the window because the wind was blowing things around.

Sister Claire was munching on a cracker when she said, «Are you absolutely sure he was the one who killed your boss?»

Elsa matter-of-factly replied, «Who else could it have been? He was the last person I saw with William. The trouble is I don›t know his name so I can›t pinpoint his identity. But in a police line-up I can probably identify him accurately. I don't know where William picks up his companions but it seems he made a fatal error on this one. I didn't know he was into this kind of activity but I did notice eyebags under his eyes which only goes to show he was up all night and didn't have enough sleep.»

Sister Claire clearly sympathized with Elsa and said, «Poor thing could›ve come to church for some counselling and spoken to a priest. Church doors are always open to the laymen to rectify their deviant ways and set them on a correct path.»

But Elsa had her doubts about the religious beliefs of William and spoke these lines, «Not everyone accepts the admonition of the church. I don›t know if William was an atheist or an unbeliever but I rarely saw him pray. There›s not even a single statue of a saint in his house. So why give him a religious memorial service? His world revolved around flamenco dancing and the dissemination of the Spanish language. I worked years for William so I›m familiar with his ins and outs and daytime visitors. As for his nocturnal exploits, I›m hardly aware. But I do know that the man I saw with William on that fateful night is most probably the assassin.» Elsa's teaspoon fell on the floor and she bent down to pick it up. After she continued, "Oh and by the way, how did things go with your visit to Mr. Salcedo, the old man in Birch St.?"

Sister Claire answered, «That frail, old man should cut down on his smoking. Never seen such a man his age smoke that much. His daughter never visits him and it›s this time of life when he badly needs company. Everytime he sees me, his eyes light up. It's as if he's never seen anyone in a long time. He gets visits from nurses once a week to check his vital signs: the blood pressure, body temperature and sugar level to see if he has diabetes. They should send him to a long-term care facility because a man with a fragile state of health is not fit to live alone. I wonder why the government doesn't look after its citizens especially now that a huge percentage of the population is ageing. At least Mr. Salcedo doesn't drink alcohol like many lonely elderly. But still his place reeks of nicotine stains and needs some general cleaning. "There was steam coming out of the tea kettle that was a sign the water was already boiling and the tea was ready to be served. They each took a cup of tea and fed on crackers spread with strawberry jam. They sat on chairs with dark red cushions and Sister Claire took a whiff from a bunch of pink roses that was placed on a vase at the center of the table. Sister Claire tried to hold a stem but pricked her finger in the process. Blood ooxzed out from her index finger and elicited a reaction. "Oh for heaven's sake. Whatever did I do?" cried Sister Claire. Elsa rushed to retrieve a box of tissue paper and dabbed some cotton swabs with alcohol to disinfect the wound. After Elsa applied merthiolet to the wound blowing it to lessen the sting. It would speed up the healing process. Later she placed a strip of band aid to protect the lesion from the elements. Elsa kept a first aid kit in the house just in case tiny incidents like this happen.

Sister Claire had fine features with skin as white as alabaster and chestnut hair that was covered by a hood because it was a requisite of her vocation. She also had hazel eyes which was a reflection of her mixed ancestry.

Sister Claire resumed the conversation where she left off. «You might want to come with me the next time I visit Mr. Salcedo. You can probably convince him to kick the habit. He›ll be so pleased to see the both of us since he enjoys the company of well-intentioned workers.»

Elsa answered, «Just ell me the exact time and date of our rendezvous, probably leave a message in my answering machine and I'll meet you at the corner of the street. I can give him some moral support in these times of uncertainty and strengthen his will to go ahead with his life. Has he ever tried to commit suicide?"

Sister Claire took a sip from her tea and replied, «He›s still standing strong inspite of the adversities. But due to the untoward succession of events, the loneliness and the excruciating solitude, he might crack up if we don't supply him with weekly visits of tender loving care. The government simply has to step in to mobilize personnel from health care services and assist patients like these with their daily needs. The government is at fault for its dereliction of duties." Elsa was jolted with surprise and said, "You can't expect anything from the government. Corruption is ingrained in the system that elected officials steal from the coffers and leave nothing for social services. That is the irony of it all. Those who were elected are the ones who are giving the citizens a hard time."

Suddenly the weather improved as correctly predicted by the forecasters. The sun peeked in the sky shining its bright rays on the damp earth with clouds drifting from west to east. There was a light breeze that blew in the same direction. Squirrels started hopping on the branches of a tamarind tree busily peeling the ripe fruit to extract some sustenance. There are many things you can do under the sun. Birds can spread their wings and preen their feathers. They can peck on the cool grass in search of grubs and worms. Two dogs were barking, a collie and a labrador retriever, because there was someone who entered the hallway leading to the apartment. Elsa buzzed her in. It was Torquata, a domestic helper who visited Elsa from time to time and who spent the days off going to movies and helping Elsa with her laundry. Panting and breathing heavily because she had to climb the stairs, Torquata began to speak, "I came here as soon as I could and want to extend my deepest condolences to you for the unexpected death of your boss. I hope the case gets resolved quickly." She brought with her a movie mazazine with a crossword puzzle at the back printed in glossy paper She handed the magazine to Elsa and said, "This is to while away your time and keep your mind focused on more constructive matters. I have a job offer in Hong Kong next month so I won't be seeing much of you. Currently there are a hundred thousand domestic workers in Hong Kong and I'm going to add to their numbers. I will join their ranks and strengthen their presence in the sphere of general services. I'm sure you'll be able to survive this hurdle." Torquata had dark lashes and her hair was brushed in a bun. She had a tawny skin coloring and wore a plain beige skirt that reached her knees. She was neat but her blouse had some coffee stains from slurping too much caffeine in the morning. She brought a can of Danish butter cookies and pretty soon all three of them were drinking tea and eating biscuits. After a brief pause, Torquata went into a tirade recounting the past week's event. "I was in a shopping mall looking at shirts in a clothing store when all of a sudden someone was tugging on the back of my blouse. I turned around and saw a six year old boy crying and looking for his mother. He told me to bring him to his mommy. I asked the store clerk if she knew the parents of the boy and she replied in the negative. I walked off the store and escorted the boy outside. I wanted to report him to the missing children's network so they could locate his parents. I figured his parents must be panicking and frantically looking for the kid. But then I decided to bring him to the nearest police station where at least they could take care of the boy while they wait for his parents. To my surprise, the police booked me for illegal abduction, physical assault and endangerment of the life to someone under the age of ten. The penalty for that kind of offense is at least five years. But I argued that they should in fact thank me for turning in the boy who was lost and deprived of the company of his parents. To my relief, after an hour or so, the mother of the boy shows up and is reunited with his mommy. The mother decides not to press any charges against me because the boy was not harmed. Next time I'll just mind my own business and leave the scene. It's not good to meddle in other people's affairs. You'll just be incriminating yourself and risk sullying your reputation in dubious circumstances."

After ruminating about what Torquata said, Sister Claire offered these words of support. "At least they didn't detain you overnight. What boggles the mind is why they didn't bother to check their database to see if you had any previous criminal record. There was no malice in your intent. Here is a woman acting in good faith and suddenly finding herself in a dispute with law enforcers. The real outlaws go scot-free as police officers just skim through their records and take no notice of their infraction. They should concentrate their efforts on the arrest of serial killers, rapists and bank robbers instead of apprehending innocent bystanders."

Elsa took out a plate of churros, crunchy rolls made of corrugated dough with chocolate syrup inside, from the refirgerator and served it with thick hot chocolate milk to her two visiting friends. "Sister Claire and I were just heading out the door toattend a church social when you came in. Do you want to come along?"

Torquata declined the invitation saying she was baby sitting tonight for her cousin's five year old son. She had a busy schedule with work almost to her neck. Keeping oneself occupied with work is a good therapy to allay feelings of depression and worthlessness. Torquata had a proposition to make as she veered toward Elsa, "Why don't you follow me to Hong Kong? I can get you an employer who'd pay you gnerously. The Chinese have a lot of money. Remember that the exchange rate is thirty pesos to one Hong Kong dollar. It's worth the try. You'll be able to buy your own home in no time."

But Elsa refused the offer, «A change of scenery would be a great relief for me but I think I›ll just stick it out here. I love my country even with all its shortcomings and pitfalls. I›m gonna miss seeing the colorful jeepneys with all its passengers crammed like sardines, the sidewalk vendors selling eggs with a grown chick inside, and the magnificent cathedrals with their ornate sculptures and statues of saints. I'm getting old and I don't think I can clean a house singlehandedly. I dream of a quiet retirement in the company of my loved ones. I may not have children of my own but I have an extended family comprising of nephews and nieces. I have them over every Christmas time."

Sister Claire scrathced her arm and soon there were red splotches on her skin. Elsa looked concerned but Sister Claire dismissed any worry on her state of health. "They're nothing serious. Just mosquito bites because we werre exposoed to the heat and humidity. We lived in a malaria infested savanna in Southern Congo. We did missionary work there running a school and a hospital for indigent families. There are so many malnourished children in Aftica that their bones are brittle and stick out from their tiny bodies. More aid is needed to be pumped into the economy to alleviate the suffering of the population. There's very little livestock from which to draw their nourishment. The drought comes and it decimates the population of cattle. Even the crops don't grow to the desired density. There's not much foliage in the landscape. Just a barren terrain with several huts made of dried mud. The literacy rate is so low that we force children to go to school. Our organization is non-profit and supply textbooks and notepads free of charge. Classes are held in makeshift tents under the blazing sun. Our hospital is in an all-out war against preventable and infectious deiseases. The nurses span out in a wide area giving away antibiotics and administering vaccines against polio, tetanus and cholera. The infant mortality rate is so high that we give specific instruction on healthy pre-natal care. One in five children die before they reach adulthood. It is a dire situation one that requires patience and stamina. You are grossly mistaken if you think all that the order of nuns does is pray and do contemplative work. We are sent overseas to depressed areas to help ease the effects of poverty. The inhabitants of these countries sorely lack the basic needs: food, water, education and clothing. We welcome doantions of any kind to reduce the severity of hunger and famine."

Elsa sought some clarification. «There›s tribal conflict in much of Africa. It›s best to avoid war-torn areas and keep out of harm›s way.»

Sister Claire answered, The war between tribes has been raging for many centuries. The warring factions are locked in battle as they claim territory from each other's jurisdiction. There are no clear boundaries and whenever their paths meet, there's bound to be a bloodbath. Civilians are caught in the crossfire and large chunks of the population fall victim to the ensuing gunfire. The list of casualties is tremendous and it is up to the aid workers to provide a safe haven to these unfortunate refugees. I know of one instance where a medical missionary was beheaded for non-payment of ransom. There are so many hoodlums within the ranks of tribal elders that its best to keep your distnace from militant groups. There are pockets of safe areas which are protected by the allied forces. This is where we conduct our business and the local population can go about their daily lives. If only the armed militia would lay down their weapons and become peace-loving members of society."

Torquata gave a piece of her mind. "That is a place where there is no rule of law. Security forces are almost non-existent and your life is in constant jeopardy from the skirmishes between opposing camps. You're safe here away from the sound of guns and grenades and you're lucky you're alive to tell your tale. Do you have any plans of going back?"

Sister Claire nodded in agreement. "It's a dangerous place out there.

Women can get raped and kidnapped as war booty. I'll leave it to the men to go into the frontlines and do the missionary work."

Elsa broached a different topic of conversation touching on the civil status of the women present. «All three of us have one thing in common, We have shunned the company of men preferring instead to lead the lives of celibacy and abnegation. We mortify our flesh when it is so tempting to roll into bed and get butt naked with the opposite sex. Sister Claire follows the path of virgin self-denial because of her religious vows, Torquata because of her dedication to a rigid work ethic and I because I'm already in my twilight years past my prime. Romantic love is only for women of a certain age bracket so they can form a famiily and untilize their God-given resources to bring forth children and propagate the human species. But we who have renounced all forms of carnal pleasure are not burdened by the complexities of motherhood nor the dire consquences of unplanned maternity. It is not to say we don't love children.

We love children except our own. Who can resist giving comfort to a weeping child or seeing them play with a ball until sunset while we sit back and reminisce of our own childhood. If we were to follow the desires of the flesh, would we would be slaves of an impure heart and putrid intentions. I never dreamed of engaging in sex. To me it sounds puerile and unrealistic. We have to mature into upright women blameless unto the law and models of propriety. We advocate for clean living leaving nothing to chance making sure we follow the path of righteousness and rectitude. We hang on to the tnets of good behaviour careful not to fall into moral turpitude. We leave behind an example of virtue and commendable qualities worthy of imitation. To sum up with what I've said, all three of us have led exemplury lives und it's time to teach the youth interpersoanl skills and a trade where they can draw a steady income and achieve economic stability."

Torquata concurred with what Elsa said and added her ideas to the conversation. "I don't want to have a man in my bed. I'm happy to sleep alone and don't want a hairy neanderthal beside me keeping me awake while he snores and makes all those lewd suggestions. I'm doing myself a faovr by keeping away from sexually transmitted diseases. Most men have multiple sex partners and can't be faithful to one woman. How long before your husband looks the other way and carries an affair with your best friend or co-worker? I'm an industrious worker cleaning houses to give it an impeccable shine. I've been approached by men who've expressed interest in me but frankly I have no time to waste on such trivial matters. What is important is to keep your boss happy and contented for a job well done. Life is not a bed of roses but requires strength and determination to surmount the hardship in life. We just can't lie down and spread our legs to earn a buck. You'll be subjecting your body to so much contagion not to mention the aggravation you risk exposing yourself to. There's no substitute for har work. It is ultimately rewarding and you'll be compensated a hundredfold if you do the job right."

It was the turn of Sister Claire to express her side of the story. «Life within the four walls of a convent is tranquil and devoid of any nuisance that can trouble the mind and the spirit. We get up early in the morning to pray and finish the day much the same way praying the vespers. Life in the enclosure is stripped down to the basics. We grow our own vegetables, make our own meals and sew our own clothes. I've grown so adept at the system that we yearn nothing more than each other's company. The only time we see a man is when a priest comes to officiate the Sunday mass. The atmosphere is so uplifiting that some nuns have had extrasensory perception and out of body experiences. Levitation, telekinesis and unexplained apparitions of saints are but a few examples of the mystical phenomena recorded in the convent. I've always believed in the supernatural. I believe there is an invisible force out there that is all-knowing and not alien to our longing for a continuation of this life. The supreme being is called by many names. But whoever He is, He is intimately allied with our deepest aspirations and our desire for eternal life. Everything happens for a reason. I am in a cloister because I like to commune with God and nature alongside people with the same affinities. I am but one of many voices who sing to the heavens. We have to renounce our baser instincts and aim for loftier goals. "Torquata took the initiative to water the indoor potted plants and ferns that lined the living room. There was a lot of sunlight that shone from above that spurred the process of photosynthesis and made the plants grow to a considerable height and dense foliage. A cat woke up from her nap and stretched her legs and limbering up while she showed off her claws. Torquata went to the refrigerator to fetch her a bowl of milk. Torquata then turned to the two women and began to narrate an incident that happened to her tow weeks ago. " i was at the front seat of a car with my brother Vincent at the wheel because we had just finished shopping for meat and fresh produce. We were enjoying the fine day taking in the sights along the way when suddenly a ten wheeler truck rammed the back of the car and created a big dent. It's a good thing I wasn't in the rear section of the car otherwise I would've borne the brunt of the impact and subsequently pinned to death. It was such a shock and the driver of the truck explained that it was due to faulty brakes. From that day onwards, my brother vowed never to drive a car again. The car was a total wreck, totally beyond repair. We could've charged the driver of the truck with criminal negligence but since we didn't sustain any injuries, we chose not to litigate."

Elsa was relieved that the incident didn›t result in bodily harm or death. She had her own tale of misfortune that she wanted to share with the group. Meanwhile, the afternoon sunlight glinted on the white streaks of her hair as she was poised to tell her story. «It was an early afternoon when I tried to cook some spare ribs for my master. I put a generous serving in the oven and decided to rest on the reclining chair. Little did I know I would fall asleep and not be able to attend to my cooking. A few hours passed and since the stove had no timer, the heat burned the spare ribs to a crisp. Smoke and toxic fumes emanated from the stove and was awaken by the nauseating odor of burnt food. I was wondering what happened and nearly fainted because of the noxious gases. I hurriedly opened the window to let the smoke out and to get some ventilation. T took out the tray of blackened spare ribs. It was incinerated beyond recognition.»

Sister Claire expressed some worry, «It›s a good thing you didn›t burn the house down.»

Elsa consoled herself at the near brush with death and offered these words of advice, «Never doze off while cooking and never use a stove without a timer. This is hardly the scenario I›d like to find myself in when I›m working. From that moment on, I purchased a fire extinguisher in case an untoward incident like this happens again.»

Sister Claire enunciated these words in relation to good housekeeping. «I never leave the tap on. Even when there is no current from the main reservoir, I make sure the faucets are turned off to avoid flooding. You have to take the necessary precautions so the house is not subject to water damage. As a rule, we only do barbecues in the garden. When there is a little get-together in the convent, we take out our equipment outdoors to avoid unnecessary inhalation of smoke. This way the place is safe and secure from emissions of greenhouse gases. As long as I›m in command, there is not one incidence of careless mishandling of tools, equipment or appliances.»

Torquata whispered in Elsa's ear, "You should take your cue from her and learn from your mistakes›"

Sister Claire resumed, «Suffice it to say, the convent is spic and span and everything is in order. You should come to me for advice on the proper maintenance of the household. You will be justly compensated if you heed my advice on measures to prevent mishaps and unlucky accidents."

Torquata caressed the feline and it purred accordingly to the light strokes of her nimble fingers. It was a tabby which was partly orange and licked the bowl of milk down to the last drop. Then Torquata uttered these words, "Have you heard of the little girl who got hit by a baseball? It was a sweltering day when a fly ball veered in her direction and landed on the soft skull of the two year old girl causing severe fractures and concussions. The baseball player showed feelings of remorse but it wasn't entirely his fault. The ball park officials have decided to build a fifteen feet high net to protect the spectators from wayward balls. They should do the same for all kinds of sports like golf, tennis and cricket. There should be a safety perimeter separating onlookers from the playing field so that no one gets hurt. Presently, the little girl is suffering from life-threatening injuries and perforations to her skull, She›s at the Children's hospital where doctors are trying to mend the immense crack on her head. That is why I don't practice sports beause you sustain a lot injuries and puts your health at risk."

Sister Claire reacted swiftly and spoke her mind. «The incident is truly unfortunate and I pray that the little girl will pull through and get better. In my younger year, before I joined the nunnery, I was a member of the women's varsity basketball team in school. I was a most valuable player shooting ten points in one game. But then the day came when I got hit by the ball right smack to my eye. I momentarily lost my eyesight as I fell to the ground waiting for medical assistance. Eventually, I went to an opthalmologist where I was informed that I developed cataracts to one eye because of the impact. I underwent an operation to remove the cataracts and to correct my blurred vision. They placed a new lens on my eye and now I see clearly. From that day on, I quit participating in sports and have since become an indoor person."

It was the turn of Elsa to talk and she spoke thus. «I was enrolled in a public school during my younger years where the tuition was subsidized by the government. Attendance was compulsory for all small children and young teenagers. I learned to read and write as they had teachers who were well-trained in their field of specialty. The school comprised of a wide area, a football field and a training ground for track and field athletes. They competed periodically in interscholastic contests. I participated in the 100 and 200 meter dash races and finished in good time. Coach Stevens trained me and gave me endurance exercises to strengthen my legs so that I can beat the clock. He gave me a pair of sneakers because the soles of my running shoes were already worn out and I was tight with money. I also joined the marathon race but gave up midway because it was too physically taxing. Sports is for men because they have the muscles that propel them to achieve great distances at a faster speed. I hate to admit it but women are the weaker sex. I didn't pursue a university education because of lack of funds. I started to work fresh out of high school.»

Torquata put the cat on her lap and started teasing it with a ball of yarn. It tried to grab the ball scratching it with her claws. She spoke, "Women are meant to be indoors, preparing meals, ironing clothes and cleaning the house. We're indispensable to the well being of men. Who can resist the charms of the housewife when she comes calling her man to the table and serves him all kinds of delicacies? But of course, we single women have a role to play too in the household. Everytime a man comes home wounded from a sport: cuts, bruises or pain in the joints, we provide basic care so they can recover from their injuries. A woman's place in a man's life cannot be ignored. We are the soothing balm that cradles men to sleep that makes them wake up refreshed, invigorated and fortified."

Torquata lay down the cat on the floor and it scampered to the other end of the room chasing what it thought was a mouse. It turned out to be the shadow of the undulating plants against the wind that blew in the room. She posed a query to Elsa, "Now that your boss is dead and you are no longer employed, what do you plan to do with so much leisure time? How do you plan to spend your days of rest and recreation?"

«Exactly that,» Elsa replied. «I saved enough money to retire comfortably. Maybe go to the river and fish for carps and catfishes. The river is teeming with marine life that we should profit from the abundance of aquatic creatures. We›re lucky the river hasn›t been polluted by chemical waste from factories that line the estuaries and deltas. I have a friend. His name is Mark Greene and he owns a motorized boat. We could ride his vessel along the choppy waters of the bay and breathe the fresh seabreeze blowing from on high. I can take selfies with my cell phone and send them to my friends. The mayor has made a great effort to preserve the pristine clarity of the river, dredging up the contaminated soil and layering it with unspoiled earth. We should tip our hats to the mayor for a job well done. He deserves to be reelected for a new four year mandate. How about you Torquata, how do you spend your days off?"

Torquata took a deep breath and answered, "I play bingo with fellow residents at the townhall and attend council meetings whenever there is an urgent matter to be resolved. I raise my hand and ask intelligent questions much to the delight of the audience who have never heard anyone talk so eloquently and pertinently. I am a member of the committee for environmental affairs and we're in charge of garbage collection, park maintenance and road safety. The prevention of accidents is our main concern. We make sure that the traffic lights are in working order and we apply fresh paint to faded crosswalks and street signs."

It was Sister Claire›s turn to contribute to the discussion and she did so with frankness and candour. "I supervise the upkeep of the convent leaving no stone unturned when it comes to maintenance and repairs. I have almost no time for myself except to pray with the novices and the abbess. We follow a rigorous schedule. We get up early in the morning to do our daily duties or household chores. After that, we buckle down and kneel before the altar and solemnly say the prayers in the missal. During our break, we cut the stems of flowers: orchids, gardenias and roses which we place in a vase to adorn our chapel. During Holy Week, we shut down our operations. We don't entertain visitors and the doors of the convent are closed to the public. We go on a little sabbatical leave sometimes extending for a period of a month. During this time we do meditation exercises, reflecting on thescriptures and examining our actions and behaviour of the recent past while on sacred ground. When the doors open after the month-long sabbatical, we welcome visitors distributing rosaries and prayer books to well-wishers and the faithful. Our convent is cloesly affiliated with the different parishes in the city. One such parish is the Archdiocese of Saint Francis. I volunteered my time and effort to handling the outreach programs so that it will bear much fruit and serve the population. And so here I am visiting senior citizens like Elsa and keeping her company. Now that she is free to spend her hours in a leisurely fashion, I invite her to come visit us in the convent and join us for some lighthearted moments and prayer."

Elsa responded with a jovial good humour, "I certainly look into that. Now that I don't have a job anymore, I can surely devote more time to ecclesiastical activities like fundraising, leading the stations of the cross on Good Friday and manning the booths that sell food during Christmas time and other feast days."

Sister Claire added these words, «I›m sure you›ll be an asset to the church. The papal nuncio would sure be glad to see you. Another soul doing God›s will on earth. It›s a quality that never goes out of style but strengthens the bond between religious officials and the laity.»Torquata was chewing on a cracker when she turned to her two friends and posed a relevant question, "Have you heard what happened lately? Well the tombstones in the Chinese cemetary have been vandalized by unidentified hoodlums who acted in the cover of night. The gravestones were sprayed with yellow paint and with a racial slur written across it that said 'Chinks go home'. As a result of that, security at the Buddhist temple has been beefed up to prevent any wanton acts of violence. The guards have been inspecting bags of worshippers and are on the lookout for any suspicious packages that may contain explosives. We are living in a dangerous era where terror attacks happen so frequently and target ethnic communities who are culturally distinct from mainstream society. I don't understand it because the Chinese are physically indistinguishable from the general population, Must be a reprisal for the persecution of religious minorities that are suffering in predominantly Buddhist countries. There is no place for racial discrimination in this country. The ethnic Chinese have contributed a lot of good to this country like the usage of the abacus and the commercial consumption of green tea and noodles. A lot of scholars have devoted their lifetime to the study of calligraphy and the teachings of Confucius which are still relevant to this day. I have been to the Buddhist temple and I must say that the ambiance there is serene and comforting. We burn incense in front of the statue of Buddha and pray before the pictures of our ancestors. The monk dressed in a gray robe with a clean shaven head leads the session with the chanting of a hymn in a monotonous tone. We sit on the floor, take off our shoes and bow our heads repeatedly while the monk leads the group in prayer. I can't understand the hostility towards the Chinese. The Chinese were here even before the Spaniards came. It's already in our DNA. The Chinese are part of our flesh and blood. We all have at least a Chinese ancestor. It's time we stop calling them names and welcome them to our family."

Sister Claire responded in this manner. «I don›t have Chinese blood since the majority of my ancestors were European. But I do sympathize with you on the plight of the ethnic Chinese in this country. The geographical location of this country should be taken into account when drawing up the civil and criminal code. The close proximity to China has only influenced us in our manner of dress, customs and traditions. We celebrate the Chinese new year with a lion dance andwe use chopsticks to eat a bowl of rice or to pick up dumplings from a steamy basket. It's all in good measure as we celebrate another facet of our rich cultural history>"

Torquata couldn't be more pleased to hear what Sister Claire said and had this to say, "Trade with China has doubled over the last ten years. The Chinese Chamber of Commerce has undertaken measures to promote bilateral relations between the two countries. The Chinese quarter is brimming with activity as merchants have sold goods to the benefit of the country. They sell herbal medicine, offer acupuncture and serve leafy vegetable and noddle soup to avid customers. I am leaving for Hong Kong and don't want this recent spate of violence to harm relations between the two countries."

Elsa expressed her opinion. «I don›t have anything against the Chinese. As a matter of fact I look to them as one of the main building blocks of our society. The others being the indio element and the hsipanic segment of the population. They're all blended into one to create a new amalgamated race. I can only wish you the best Torquata in your endeavour to improve your economic situation. May your trip to Hong Kong be richly rewarding and may you be able to build a prosperous life." Torquata interrupted Elsa and had this to say. "The Chinese president is slated to make an official visit to the country and I am at the forefront of the welcoming committee. It's the least I can do to show my appreciation for the warm reception I'll be getting in Hong Kong. I am leaving as a migrant worker and all my papers are in order. I expect to be truly compensated by this undertaking."

Sister Claire applied lip gloss to her dry, chapped lips and drank a glass of ice cold water, a relief from the hot and humid weather that has enveloped the city. She introduced a new subject matter to their conversation. «It›s painful to see people living in the street with no home to call their own. Young men with auditive and cognitive faculties that are fully functional but are unable to find employment. With the legalization of cannabis, a lot of youth just sit and loiter in the park taking puffs from that noxious substance. They›re juvenile deliquents who need help and guidance. The smell from cannabis is fctid and bitter and makes me cringe everytime I see idle youths inhale from those harmful cigarettes. They should know that marijuana is dangerous to the health and induces altered states of the mind. The young people can never recover from their addiction to marijuana and needs a swift, decisive action from the government. The government should rescind the bill legalizing cannabis because it only promotes laziness and depravity."

Elsa shook her head and added these words, «There are drugs which are more lethal than cannabis. The use of fentanyl by the homeless youth has spiked in recent years increasing the mortality rate of drug overdose. There›s an opioid crisis in the city today that needs to be resolved. Dirty syringes and blood splattered pieces of clothing are strewn in city streets as a sign of the growing problem with narcotics. Police officials should pursue drug dealers to the full extent of the law and prosecute them in criminal courts. Our laws should be more stringent imposing the death penalty to drug traffickers who seek to ruin the lives of our youth. The young people are the hope of tomorrow. If we don›t improve their lot in life and protect them from vicious habits, we›ll be left in the doldrums unable to foster a productive society. Cocaine and heroin are two drugs which should be stamped out from the face of the earth and cannabis should only be used for medicinal purposes. The priorities of this government are misaligned. Ever heard of the customs official who sold seized cocaine on city streets and earned a million bucks? The officers who are sworn to protect us are the ones who are endangering our health. The building will smell if they let residents smoke cannabis or cigarettes in their homes. Eviction notices and termination of lease should be served to tenants who fail to comply with a smoke-free environment. There was a tenant who incessantly smoked in his apartment and he was kicked out by the bailiff for non-compliance of the city ordinance. Not to mention the cigarette butts they litter on the streets and parks that the cleaning brigade has to sweep away every so often."

Torquata adjusted her collar and nodded in agreement. "Aside from that, smoking is a fire hazard. A lot of fires have been started by lit cigarettes. One has to dispose of cigarettes properly in ashtrays or trash bins. There's a raging forest fire south of the country. One can only hope for rain to put out the fire. Not to mention the smog that these brush fires emit. Already there is a smoky haze that is jeopardizing the health of people with respiratory ailments. It is unbearably hot in the city and the greenhouse gases are trapped in the earth's atmosphere. The excessive heat generated by the brush fires stifles the natural flow of the air. The wind is worsening the situation as it fans the flames and increases the intensity of the heat. You shouldn't exert too much physical exercise as it only increases the likelihood of a stroke."

Elsa added these words, «That is why I use light, skimpy clothing when going outside. There is no air conditioning and the heat is tremendous. I don›t see how Sister Claire can wear a nun›s habit all day considering the heat wave we›re experiencing.»

Sister Claire answered Elsa, «The material of the dress I wear is light and flimsy. I bring a fan with me wherever I go. I›ve gotten used to this outfit and it is a rule of the convent that I wear it as a uniform.»

Torquata continued the topic of conversation and had this to say, "Five people have died so far in the ongoing heat wave. The extreme weather is taking it's toll on the population. People should head to resource centers to avail themselves of free air conditiong. It is important to drink plenty glasses of water and stay hydrated for the remainder of the day. The exhaust fumes from cars, buses and factories are to blame for the increasein temperature. People become lethargic and do not want to use physical effort because of the suffocating heat. The polar ice caps are melting and the sea levels are rising. Soon those island in the South Pacific and Indian ocean will be submerged with water. Inhabitants have to go to higher elevation where they can be safe from inundations."

Sister Claire had this to say. «If you think the situation is bad here, you should see what›s happening in the northern hemisphere. Their winter months have never been so brutal. They have record snowfalls that have clogged roads and highways. Snow removal operations are slow as emergency crews are dispatched to ease traffic jams. The sleet and ice on the road have produced vehicular accidents and monstrous pile ups. Subzero temperatures are occurring more frequently as countries scramble to supply enough electiricty from the power grid. Hydro electric companies are at the verge of a breakdown as consumers complain of insufficient power supply, power outages and faulty connections. People are clothed in thick goose down jackets complete with scarves, mittens and hats as they trudge through more than a foot of snow that has fallen on the ground. Flights in airports have been cancelled due to blizzard conditions and poor visibility. There is a backlog of passengers who have to rebook. Everywhere you go, there is an anomaly of weather conditions. People have to change their habits because the gas they consume is doing a lot of harm. Carbon dioxide emissions have risen in the past decade and contributes to the changing weather pattern. The rise in the price of oil has compounded the problem as electric consumption has become expensive and out of reach by the ordinary household."

Continuing this line of thought, Elsa said, «Because of climate change, typhoons are getting stronger. It was only recently when we had a category 5 hurricane packing winds of up to 220 kph. It tore through houses, trampling dwellings like a box of matches. The roofs of buildings were pulled apart as yachts in the marina were tossed and upturned. The waves in the sea were rough and strollers were cautioned to stay indoors and not venture outside where winds could wipe you off your feet.»

Torquata uttered a prophecy. "We are in the throes of another global meltdown. If men don't reduce their emissions of heat and pollution, the whole earth will be dry and parched unable to grow any edible food. Trees will shrink in size due to the poor quality of the soil. Flowers will wither as they don't receive enough nutrients. The whole world will be a drab place to live in. People should switch to electric cars or hybrid vehicles. Aside from their insignificant consumption of gas, they're sleek and quieter to maneuver. Our driving habits won't be affected by the fluctuating price of oil if we go electric. The instability of the gulf region has only created an atmosphere of strife and uncertainty. We have to resort to cleaner energy fuels like wind, geothermal, hydro electric dams and solar panels. We have to harness other sources of energy that don't pollute the environment. Sadly and as of this moment, industrialized countries continue to import large quantities of oil to supply power to their factories and assembly lines. We have to be free form our dependency to oil by upgrading our machinery so it runs on alternative sources of energy."

Sister Claire deviated from the topic and offered instead these pointers on etiquette. «When sitting at a dinner table, always make sure you have a napkin on your lap or folded across your chest. Try not to spill food or bread crums. You can wipe them away with the napkin or gently put them at the corner of your plate for later disposal. If you are wearing lipstick, wipe it thoroughly with a napkin so you don't leave marks on the glasses. The napkin will preferably be the color white so you can see clearly the residue you discard. Never use strong perfume that might be offensive to the olfactory sense of your seatmate. A light scented cologne is preferable to sweeten the ambiance at the dinner table. Never use a toothpick to clean your teeth in the presence of other guests. It is regular practice among Chinese nationals but is definitly not suitable for our daily routine. Use a spoon that is convex when you drink your soup. Never slurp or make those gurgling noises because it is revolting and impolite. You have to be considerate with your seatmate giving them enough elbow room to maneuver while serving the food. If you are an early bird or arrive before the appointed time, stay in the foyer and have a drink with some canapes while conversing with the hostess."

Torquata reacted. "You're a well-rounded person with a lot of things going for you. You obviously learned these rules in the convent where the nuns demostrate good behaviour and decorum. But in this country, the masses eat without utensils. They like to sccop up the rice with shards of fish and push it into their mouths. There's nothing you can do to change this practice. People sit on the floor and wipe their mouths with their shirts. Some use banana leaves and put their food on it dispensing with the spoons and forks as they handle the food with their bare hands. Anyway, you have to use your hands when eating fish that hasn't been deboned and remove the tiny needles that can choke you if you accidentlly swallow them. What the people in this country like to eat is a shrimp pase that emits a foul smell and is offensive to the senses. They ear it as a sauce or a side dish to liven up the main course. You've lived here long enough to know the habits of the people. I wonder why you're not used to it."

Sister Claire retorted. «I am perfectly aware of the customs of the people here. Just because the majority of the people do it, doesn›t mean it›s right. We have to educate the masses on the principles of hygiene and good manners. I am also aware that people cook their food on earthenware pots over a coal powered portable stove which is not right. It is advisable to cook your food using an appliance to prevent from buring your meal that can be carcinogenic when consumed. You can regulate the temperature better that way. Otherwise, it's like living in the stone age."

Sister Claire continued her lecture. "Never burp while eating. Chew your food well and never feel as if you're being rushed because this will only lead to unfortunate consequences. Always take your time to enjoy the food, savoring the flavors as it gently dissolves in your mouth. If you have to talk on the table, make sure you have fully digested the food before you utter a word. Never talk when your mouth is full. If you have to stand up from the talbe, ask that you may be excused and gently push your chair to the table. Never abruptly leave without saying a word."

Elsa boiled some water in the kettle so her friends could have some more tea. She toasted some bread so they could have it with jam. She had this to say, «I only have paper napkins. I have nothing planned for dinner as I usually take out Chinese food. My cups and saucers are made of blue china while my knives and forks are stainless steel.»

Sister Claire noticed the pretty designs on the cups and exclaimed, «Dainty little cups you have here. I admire you for your cleanliness. Everything is in their proper place. It is indeed more economical to use paper napkins and disposable plastic water bottles as refreshments.»

But Torquata stuck to her guns and pursued her line of thinking. "The trouble with you Europeans is you take us for granted. You sit back and relax while we natives work our butts out as we till the soil and make crops grow. The date of our civilization is nebulous but long before the European settlers came here, we were already building boats. We rode the waves to each and every island populating the country and taming the wilderness. You people think we still live in trees, but we developed an advanced culture that can rival other geographical jurisdictions. For instance, we formulated our own alphabet that we wrote in the trunks of banana trees. It's a cursive script so as not to rupture the delicate texture of the banana trunk. We drafted our own code of ethics that is still the model of many systems of conduct. You instituted you own laws in this country while you ignore the fact that we already reached a high level of jurisprudence. We are a very practical people. We build nipa huts with bamboo floors and thatched roofs for better ventilation of the living quarters. We live in a tropical climate so cement blocks are not suitable material. It is so relaxing to lie your head down on bamboo slats with only a straw mat to serve as a padding. Bamboo floors are supple and flexible which is beneficial to people with back pain and arthritis.

Our women wore colorful fabrics that we weaved in wooden looms. Our men wore sparse clothing to better aerate the body in this hot, searing weather. We dug wells that oveflow with water which we carry in buckets for our daily needs. Our political system was divided into fiefdoms that was headed by a chief who oversaw the welfare of the people. We didn't have a concept of a country then but since there was no tribal conflict, there was no need for an army. We were living in peace and tranquility until you settlers came and wrested control over our domain. You introduced scarcity of food and pestilence. Through your agrarian reform you took control of vast tracts of land. And you expect us to kowtow to the colonial master after you've drained us of our wealth and deprived us of what is rightfully ours. All this talk about etiquette is only a facade that hides the brutal force by which you conquered us."

Elsa rushed to settle the dispute and placed herself between the two opposing parties. She tried to calm the nerves of both women and had this to say. «Now, let›s not get carried away and hurl tart statements at one another. Both of you have made valuable pointers on the different aspects of everyday life.

Sister Claire is explaining the dos and donts of table manners while Torquata is tracing the trajectory of an ancient civilization that is still practiced today. We differ from each other in significant ways and what is acceptable to one might not be admissible to the other. There is really no right or wrong in this case. We live according to what is handed to us from one generation to the other. It doesn't matter whether you are uncouth or have unsophisticated demeanor. What matters more is that you're a law-abiding citizen and follows the norms of society. You haven't broken the law if you eat with your bare hands or make strange noises on the talbe. But let us not look at each other condescendingly just because she behaves in a peculiar fashion."

Sister Claire tried to reconcile herself with Torquata in a forthright manner. "We must not pander to our basic instincts that can degenerate our outlook on life. Man does not live in caves anymore but has emerged into a whole new light and not be amiss on our standard practices. Since we live in the upper echelons of society, it is expected of us to follow certain standars of behaviour. You can very well do what you please, but let us not test each other's patience by grating into the car of decent noblemen."

Torquata coughed and sneezed into a handerkerchief. She remarked,

"Must be my allergies. When there's too much smog in the air, I produce an adverse reaction." She coverred her mouth while she did this.

Sister Claire reacted. «At least you›re getting the gist of the matter. You covered your mouth when you coughed which is a sign that you›re an educated woman and you don›t want to spray your saliva to other people. Keep it up and soon other people will look up to you and yearn for your companionship.»

Elsa put on a pair of blue denims and a silky blouse with floral print. She brushed her hair and put it in place with a fancy clip. All three of them went down the stairs and exited the building. Sister Claire and Elsa bade goodbye to Torquata who headed off in the other direction. Sister Claire and Elsa walked in the balmy afternoon towards St. Francis church where they would be joined by a few other parishioners.

Sister Claire and Elsa arrived at the church of St. Francis just in time for the 5 o›clock Saturday mass. The priest was making an entrance at the center aisle of the church with the deacon holding the Bible aloft in his hands. There were small children, eucharistic ministers and lecturers of the gospel who preceded the priest as they marched to the altar.

The choir was singing at the top of their voices which was comprised of sopranos, tenors, mezzos and baritones. They wore formal outfits to give the church a dignified appearance. There was a microphone perched on top of the choir to better capture the sonority of the voices. A man played the organ as the choir sang haymns from loose leaflets distributed by a member. The organ was refurbished by an expert technician and was in perfect pitch. Stained glass windows adorned the altar of the church which reflected the sunlight into many hues. There were statues of saints carved in white marmara marble with votive candles in the front. Sister Claire and Elsa sat in one of the pews in front of the church the better to hear the priest deliver his sermon. The priest spoke of forgiveness for one's enemies, not seeking revenge for the harm done. He spoke of love for the fellowman because war is just a vicious cycle that drains a person emotionally. The priest was wearing a white tunic with symbols of the church embroidered in the front. The sermon of the priest struck a chord in Elsa who sought justice for the brutal slaying of her master. There would be no rest until reparation for the crime committed would come to pass. The priest lifted the golden chalice and everyone knelt down to partake of the supper of the Redeemer. The voices of the choir rose to hit the topmost note then ebbed as the cadence came to a close. The singing will resume during the recessional hymn. Elsa and Sister Claire along with the rest of the congregation took holy communion except the young children who were too young to understand.

After the mass, Sister Claire and Elsa exchanged pleasantries with the priest. The priest who officiated the mass was Father Onyema who came from Uganda. He lamented the dwindling number of parishioners who attend mass especially in northern countries. A lot of priests from Africa were being summoned by the headquarters in the Vatican to perform ecclesiastical duties in northern countries. Only a few men in these countries have pondered about joining the hierarchy of priests. Not too many recruits that is why African priests were called to fill in the ranks of religious leaders. Father Onyema wanted to inspire devotion to the blessed sacrament among the laymen and urge them to take up a priestly vocation. You'll be amply rewarded if you enter the religious life because there are so many people who yearn for spiritual healing. Especially in strife-torn countries cooler heads should prevail. There must be an arbiter who will weigh all arguments carefully and consider the best option to resolve the conflict. He must be a person who is not affiliated to a political party and who can lead peace-keeping operations with support from missionaries and religious co-workers. He must spread peace and goodwill. An ambassador who will represent the pope in the various functions of the church. He should address the root causes of strife and division while protecting the lives of women, children and other vulnerable members of society. He should reconcile religious differences bridging the gap betwen minority groups and mainstream practitioners. He should ask more affluent countries to open their doors to refugees who suffer from religious persecution and economic deprivation. The leader must strive to eradicate racial prejudice which undermines the equal opportunities given to each citizen and curtails their rights to a decent livelihood. He must be a man of impeccable credentials having risen from the ranks of community work to settling disputes between warring entities. He must have prior experience with the diplomatic corps resolving deadlocks and bringing an end to crises.

We should give each man the opportunity for employment and reward him according to his talents and work output.

Sister Claire and Elsa descended the stairs leading to a small cubicle in the interior of the church. The room was large enough to seat thirteen people around a rectangular table. They were greeted by the organizer of the Legion of Mary whose name was Margaret Ortigas. She welcomed Sister Claire with open arms because they already knew one another. Margaret said, "I see you brought a friend with you. We never tire having new members attend our group meeting. People come and go but we remain steadfast to our principles of piety and religious devotion."

There was a statue of the Virgin Mary at the end of the table surrounded by a few lit candles which gave the air of solemnity and reverence.

Sister Claire answered Margaret›s inquiry. «This here is Elsa. She lives not far from here and is an old acquaintance of mine with whom I visit every so often to keep her company. She recently went through a dreadful ordeal and wondered whether a prayer group like this can uplift her spirit..."

Elsa spoke, «I am not a regular churchgoer but I had a religious upbringing and am familiar with the doctrines of the church. I›ve been having bad dreamsand flashbacks lately and am wondereing whether prayer can put an end to it."

Margaret looked up from the ledger book she was reading and answered Elsa. «Prayer can definitely help you. But before we begin praying we are given time to introduce ourselves and have conversations with each other so that we can better have an idea about who we›re dealing with. Later, a priest comes into the room and leads us to say the rosary. The only requirement is that we give the church a chance to improve our lives.»

Elsa scratched her head and asked, «Are we the only ones who›ll be attending this meeting? Where›s the rest of the people?»

Margaret answered, «We start in thirty minutes. You›ll be surprised by the number of people who›ll be coming. In the meantime, you can read this book which is a brief synopsis of the life and times of our founder, Fr. Ernesto Sanchez. He was a franciscan friar who oversaw the construction of this church calling on architects to use stone and mortar exclusively so that this building is impervious to fires, earthquakes and floods. The church dates back to the mid-nineteenth century when the majority of the population had already been converted to the Catholic faith. This church was the scene of many historical events like the promulgation of the edict of Claveria which bestowed hispanic surnames to natives. The recent bomb attack on a church in the southern part of the country has shaken and deeply saddened us because we are a close-knit community even in far-flung rural areas. The ones who carried out the attack don't deserve a second chance at life. A just punishment will be handed out to them and they will be sent to the gallows where they will meet their fate for reparation of their crimes. All we ask from citizens is their adherence to the rules and regulations of the church which is in strict compliance with the laws of the land. We protect the sanctity of human life by outlawing abortion and prohibit the mockery of marriage by restricting it to two people of the opposite sex. Under no circumstances will we condone same-sex marriages and no priest will perform the ceremony uniting two people of the same gender. We have a lobby group in congress that is working to discourage the passage of a similar bill. We are not affiliated with the government but throughout history, we played a pivotal role in the development of society."

Elsa was curious to know as to who was behind the deadly bomb attacks that tore through a church while the mass was in progress and killed 22 people.

Margaret answered with a serious face and lines on her forehead that they were probably Muslim extremists who are fighting for an independent homeland. No arrests have been made as of this date as the suspects seem to be hiding in the rugged terrain in the southern part of the country. They target innocent civilians and detonate bombs in crowded places to inflict more damage and casualties. The group known as the Abu Sayyaf has claimed responsibility for the attack and has been labeled a terrorist group by the U.S. embassy. The Muslim population of the island inhabits a volatile region where the murder rate has risen dramatically in recent years. The government has sought to quell the insurrection by declaring martial law and imposing a curfew whereby people will be safer in the streets. People are reluctant to leave their homes because they fear hoodlums might retaliate due to the tense situation and the heightened police surveillance. The autonomous Muslim region has been given more powers by the government in the administration of their affairs. But many Muslim leaders have argued that this step is not satisfactory because it is only a superficial measure that does not solve the ills besetting the region. High unemployment, an acute shortage of hospital staff and insufficient manpower are only some of the problems that have affected the region. Muslim separatists are clamoring for an independent state which they say will foster closer ties with wealthy Muslim countries, alleviate poverty and establish their identity as a proud Muslim nation.

But the federal government has refused to grant concessions saying that the southern region is part and parcel of the country. The Muslim segment of the population is one of the two founding peoples that have helped shape the destiny of the country. The perception Catholics have of Muslims are askew and unfair. Many muslims complain of discrimination when it comes to hiring practices of leading corporations. Big corporations that rake in huge profits like television networks, beverage and hotel conglomerates, and airline companies are controlled by Chinese taipans and local oligarchs who have no connection to the Muslim world. The wealth of the country should be distributed equally to all the people and not concentrate it on one sector of society. But only a splinter group supports Muslim secession. The majority have no qualms about staying with the federation.

Elsa rose to make a comment, «We should step forward and seek an end to the bombings. We can show solidarity by putting on a brave face and march through the streets clamoring for an end to hostilities. We can seek greater cooperation from our Muslim neighbors so they can rein in on the rebellious elements of the population. An economic alliance with our richer southern neighbors can decrease unemployment, diffuse the tension and usher in a new era of friendship.»

Sister Claire offered these words of comfort, «What matters more is that this place is safe and secure from terrorists. Discontent is only widespread in the southern islands of the country and no rebels have been known to inflict harm on churches here. But you have a point. Our armed forces are doing their utmost to eradicate the menace to the well-being of the citizens. It doesn›t matter what religion you practice as long as you treat your fellowman with love, understanding and compassion. These are the basic teachings that the church espouses.»

After a brief break, Elsa posed this question, "What can you say about the scandals that have rocked the church?"

Margaret answered, «The repercussions of these incidents are grave and far-reaching. The scandals have seriously affected our reputation as an entity for the commom good. One such priest was Fr. Geighan. He was accused of abusing a boy during one of his trips overseas. The circumstances surrounding the event are murky and the testimonies were inconsistent. Nevertheless, to save the church from further embarrassment, we reached a financial settlement with the boy's family sparing the priest from a prison sentence. The priest was subsequently defrocked and is no longer associated with the archdiocese. We urge anyone to report any suspicious activity happening on church grounds. We don't coddle erring priests but surrender them to authorities so they can be charged and prosecuted. Fortunately fior us, inspite of this one incident, we were able to recoup our losses, derive income from our various outreach programs, gather much needed financial support from our weekly collections and regain the trust of our parishioners."

Elsa added, «But the situation of the church in North America is worse than here where the priests have committed a serious injustice to the population. Think of the residential schools of the First Nations communities where they snatched children from their mothers and indoctrinated them with a culture alien to their own. These children were forced to stand in a corner and had to endure corporal punishment because they wouldn›t obey. They were forbidden to speak their own language and their manner of dress was altered to conform to western standards. How can you justify that?»

Margaret responded, «You are very well-informed. Cases of abuse like this have been well documented in the annals of the church. The church has admitted its wrongdoing and the ecumenical council in Rome has issued an apology. But words of apology are not enough to placate the resentment felt by the victims. This is merely lip service. The church has sought to indemnify the victims by acknowledging the harm done to them. There is a financial package available to compensate for the injustice that was incurred by the priests. There have been mass demonstrations in front of the Vatican calling for a top to bottom clean up of the church and the resignation of church officials. We live in a democratic society where everyone is free to express his opinion. But the pontiff has refused to grant them an audience saying they should direct their grievances to the proper channels. The pope has said that those men who constantly attack the church are allied with the devil and who seek to destabilize the church down to its core."

Elsa continued asking questions. «Perhaps you can urge the church to ordain female priests so there can be more equality within its ranks?»

Margaret gave this stern reply, «Let›s face it. The church is a male-dominated institution dating back to its inception 2,000 years ago. We are not in a position to ask questions about the hierarchy of the church. It›s just the way it is. A woman›s place is subservient to a priest and is not fit to administer the sacraments. Only male priests are allowed to perform nuptial rites and hear confessions from the faithful. But women are allowed to lead the extra curricular activities of the church under the supervision of a priest. Women are best suited to do secretarial work and the upkeep and maintenance of the church. But when it comes to the handling of the church's finances, it's best left to the priest who will see to it that there is proper funding for the various outreach programs."

Elsa asked yet another question, "What about gay couples who want to legitimize their union? The state has already recognized the validity of such unions granting them the right to possess conjugal properties, shared custody of children and the right to bequeath wealth to the designated widower. Yet the church refuses to extend their blessings to same sex couples. Isn't it time for a change?"

Margaret responded, «Marriage is a sacrament that is a bond between two people of the opposite sex. Once the marriage is consummated, nothing can tear them asunder. Homosexuality is a deviant sexual behaviour that is an abominable act in the eyes of the church. You have to abide by the accepted norms to avail yourself of the benediction of the church. Politics and religion are separate. Not all things that are legal are accepted by the church. We know that a great number of people have an outlook on life that is lopsided and non-conventional. People accuse us of being prejudicial to homosexuals but that has been our position since the beginning of time. Remember the time when God rained down sulphuric acid on the inhabitants of Sodom and Gomorrah? They were people with loose morals and practiced unimaginable acts of adultery and fornication. Their heathen culture so offended God that he punished them severely with a wave of his hand. Homosexuals are a promiscuous people who have contracted many diseases like AIDS and sexually transmitted illnesses. We preach that couples remain monogamous and be faithful to their partners. Marital infidelity can cause the break up of a marriage resulting in a lot of hurt and psychological torment. There is no place for homosexuals in the church. They should repent of their sin and follow the path of righteousness."

But Elsa asked further, «There will be a pride parade through a long route in the city. There will be floats with scantily-clad men showing off their muscles dancing to the beat of the samba. It›s a crowd drawer, one that grabs the headlines in newspapers and TV.»

Margaret answered stoically, «Such revelry is an offshoot of pagan culture. People line the streets to catch a glimpse of the party-goers. Even representatives of the government will be in attendance in this much publicized event. To the chagrin of the religious community, the gay population is growing at a fast pace.

The political candidates who take part in the festivities are there only to garner votes and win in the election. We plead with our leaders to show some restraint when it comes to participation in this immoral celebration."

Elsa argued further, «But it›s a fun-filled event, one that does no harm to anyone. Sex between two consenting adults is legal and there should be nothing that can hamper its happy ending.»

But Margaret refuted Elsa›s claims. «Sex should only be practiced within the framework of marriage. Procreation by couples should be the goal of any sexual activity. Men and women who choose not to get married should remain celibate the rest of their lives much like priests who have taken a vow of chastity."

Elsa squarely replied, «Don›t worry Margaret. I am a single woman who has renounced all forms of intimacy with the opposite sex. I just wanted you to clarify some of the issues that have as yet been clouded in doubt. I just wish the church would be more flexible and give some leeway to our children so they can all have some fun and enjoy themselves.»

Margaret then made this assertion, «Everything you do should be for the glory of God and not for the hedonistic pleasure of men.»

The guests started to trickle into the chamber where the meeting was to be held. First up was Lina Duvalier, a blonde blue-eyed buxom beauty with oversized breasts but with slim buttocks and thighs. The idea of her joining a religious meeting was laughable since she didn›t exude any holy charms. She would fit more snugly in a western sitcom dancing with one foot up around a teepee waiting for some cowboys to make a fire for cooking beans and a wild bison, their catch for the day. But there she was wearing a tight-fitting dress with a plunging neckline that showed a hefty portion of her flesh. She wore a diamond brooch with emerald studs on her lapel.

Elsa made a caustic remark, «How›d you manage to walk in here without people noticing your sexy curves and voluptuous allure? You›re more suited to be in a beer garden serving drinks to rowdy male customers.»

Linda replied, «When I was working in a fastfood outlet, men whould flock to the counter to fondle my breasts. I willingly obliged because that way I caught their attention and sold more sizzling steaks and hors d'oeuvres. The manager kept me for an indefinite period of time because he considered me a valuable asset to the company.

But with all the rush to make a buck, I didn't have inner peace. There was this void in my spirit I knew could only be filled by prayer with other people. So here I am, trying to make amends for my past transgressions."

Elsa made a suggestion. «It would be better if you covered up a little. You›re showing too much cleavage which may be an occasion of sin.» Elsa took a black vest from the clothes rack and handed it to Linda. «Here, put this on. You›re revealing too much of your body. You›re catering to the animal instincts which is not the goal of this group.»

Linda replied, «I›ll gladly put this vest on on the condition that you let me sit beside the priest. It's not everyday that you get a blonde woman attending your meeting. I'll inspire the priest and the congregation to pray more fervently. I'm here to spice things up. A much needed break from the dull gray clouds that are looming in the horizon. You'll attract more people to the fold if you station pretty girls like me at the church doors inviting strangers to come in. More and more people of color are filling the pews in the church and not many white folks seem to be biting the bait. You should serve God in your best apparel and put your best foot forward.

The gospel says everything for the greater glory of God. How can we attain that level of distinction if the people running the church lack the requisite good looks?"

Sister Claire made this assertion, "Love is blind. You don't judge a man by the color of his skin but by what he utters. If you hear a calling from God then by all means enter through the narrow door. For many have chosen to lead dissolute lives and their hearts are impure, covered in grime and evil intentions. People who are imbued with a religious zeal should follow the footsteps leading to salvation. What good is it if a white man comes into the church but shows no regret for his offenses? Better a man of color whose heart has been cleansed and whose actions are inspired by divine powers."

Pointing to the brooch, Elsa inquired sarcastically, «Where›d you get that, from whoring around?»

Linda was in the defensive and replied, «My father was the CEO of a large multinational corporation. We live in a comfortable home with a whole range of cars and all the amenities. Something that you›ll never have.»

Elsa answered back, «At least I›m not followed by malicious men because of some distorted breasts.»

Linda replied directed at Elsa, «There›s something about your face that turns off men. Maybe you should have surgery to correct your facial abnormalities.

Elsa was nervously fidgeting with her rosary running her fingers up and down the beads. She took out a bottle of water from her bag and took a long, hard gulp to quench her thirst. Elsa took a close look at Linda who seemed unperturbed by her snide remarks. She replied, «Men aren›t interested in me and I›m not interested in them. I am an example of modesty, cut out from all the sensual pleasures of the world. I know the kind of woman you are (unsmiling and intense). You lounge in bed and masturbate for hours. You hop into bed with any man you meet as often as you change your clothes. In spite of the fact that you go to church, you›re a wolf in sheeps's clothing. You're an easy lay who gets a kick out of tempting men to do licentious things. Tell me, when was your last sexual encounter with men. Last night or the night before? Women like you should be kept under lock and key so you don't infect the world with your lecherous ways."

Margaret butted in the raging conflict positioning herself between the two women who were trading barbs with one another. «Everyone is welcome to enter the church because we are committed to serving the community. If you search your conscience you'll be able to hear the voice of God exhorting you to be respectful of his commandments. All we ask is that you come in a decent attire. No thongs or slippers and no skimpy outfits that can deflect our attention from the gospel."

Linda interjected this comment. «But the heat is unbearable and we›ll be sweating profusely if we don›t wear the least clothing possible. We›ll be fainting and lose consciousness if we don›t adapt to the hazardous effects of the blazing summer. We even need umbrellas to shield ourselves from the hot rays of the sun.»

Margaret acquiesced to Linda›s suggestion. «In that case, you can come in any way you want. We don›t want people collapsing in the middle of a service. If you suffer from dizziness, better to stay at home and take some rest. If you are unable to get up from your bed, a member of the clergy will visit you at home to pray with you and give you absolution of sins.»

But Linda didn›t want to let go of Elsa as she had these sharp, acrid comments directed at her. «I don›t know why you›re so jealous of me. Men stare at me because of my provocative appearance.

They open doors for me and offer a seat in a crowded bus or subway. Once in a bar, a man offered me a glass of sparkling wine and sought my presence at his table. We chatted the night away but reached a conclusion that we'd just be firends. I noticed a ring on his finger and he turned out to be a married man but that his wife was unresponsive to his needs. I left him like a hot potato because I'm not a homewrecker. I only go out with single, unattached men. I don't want to cause the break up of a family, leave the rightful wife forlorn and sobbing. So you see Elsa, I do have a conscience and I choose with whom I flirt with."

Sister Claire chimed in, «Look at me. I am fully clothed and not an inch of my body is exposed. Even my hair is covered to discourage people from taking a good look at me. I have given up the worldly life to devote my whole time in the service of the church. But of course, I am cognizant of the fact that only a few women have the vocation to pursue a religious life. Without the church, I am like a lost sheep looking for the rest of the herd so I can safely enter the kingdom of God. (Referring to Linda) Maybe your time will come too when you will shed your provocative looks and start mortifying your flesh.»

Other guests started to enter the cubicle. One such guest was Fatima Hassan, a young Muslim woman who was wearing a dark hijab. She was carrying a leather-bound copy of the Koran, the Muslim holy book. She was fair-skinned and her features were typically arabic. She was also carrying worry beads which was different from the rosary because it didn't have a religious connotation. She faced Margaret and the rest of the interlocutors. "Hello, my name is Fatima. I am a Muslim woman who is visiting this church for the first time. I am overwhelmed by the number of churches in the city, It seems that there is a church for each borough. Like a good and curious neighbor, I have come to familiarize myself with the rituals of your church. Conversion to your religion is, however, out of the question as I am a devout Muslim woman whose outlook on life is vastly different from yours. The Koran is a book we read everyday and learn from the pithy aphorisms stated therein. There are only two mosques in the whole city and they are usually filled to the rafters with worshippers kneeling on the floor and bowing their heads in prayer. As a gesture of goodwill, I invite everyone to come witness first-hand our manner of worship.

The faith of your brothers down south is Islam. And there is a great divide that separates us due to ignorance and biased reporting. It is not true that most Muslims are terrorists or harbor ill-feelings towards America or other western countries. We'd like to be your partners in nation building so there will be a brighter tomorrow for everyone. The treatment that Muslims have received in this country is harsh and uncalled for. Why has the president declared martial law on our part of the island? How can we go about our lives if so many restrictions have been placed on us? We want to exercise our right to peaceful assembly and let our voices be heard. We want to show to the authorities that we have been hurt by the diatribes spewed forth by the leaders of this country. It is not right to call us names (like Muslim pigs) or to bar us from boarding an aircraft on the suspicion of trying to blow up the plane. The Middle East, where I originally come from, is beset with social and political problems. But you cannot just dump us in the trash heap because we hold vast reserves of oil which are indispensable to your cars, planes and industries. What we ask is better treatment of your Muslim brothers. You have curtailed our rights by refusing to recognize our distinct culture that we have sought to preserve and nurture. You have treated us.

like second-class citizens because the size of our population is only a fraction of yours. If talks fail at the bargaining table then there is no other choice but to pursue our goal through violent means. As of this moment, there are too many foreign powers interfering with our internal affairs. We won't be subservient to colonial masters who are depleting our natural resources and leaving us bone-dry through the mismanagement of oil rigs."

Margaret interrupted Fatima. «The problem is your system of government. The sheikhs, sultans and kings who rule your countries are not elected officials. What you need is a democratically elected government. In the meantime, those power hungry demagogues will continue to fleece the economy with every cent they can. With international organizations like OPEC, we can standardize oil production and regulate the price of oil so it doesn›t appear volatile on the world market. The world economy is at a tailspin due to the instability of the Middle East. You only have yourselves to blame for your bad reputation as crime-infested and terror-ridden countries. In this part of the country, terror-related offenses have been sporadic thanks largely to predominantly Catholic population that comprises one cohesive unit. But you stay here and observe the manner we do things. You›ll be enthused by the warm reception you›ll get from the faithful.»

So many questions were swirling in Linda's mind about the Arab world that they landed at the tip of her tongue. She mustered up enough courage and asked Fatima to explain some debatable topics. "Why is homosexuality a crime in Arab countries when consensual sex between two adults regardless of gender is safe and legal in many other countries?

It is no business of law enforcement officers to pry into the bedrooms of people and find out what is going on. As long as the minimum age requirement is met then individuals should be free to show their love for one another. We should not impede people from enjoying each other's company as long as they practice safe sex to stop the spread of the AIDS virus. It has always been the objective of Planned Parenthood to promote safe sex and keep away unwanted pregnancies by distributing prophylactics. In Brunei, for instance, homosexuality is a crime punishable by death. There is an outcry from various agencies that this is a blatant violation of human rights. Since when did the intimacy of same-sex couples who cuddle and hug one another in the privacy of their own room pose a danger to society? Instead of going after corrupt elements who gouge out every penny the people have, they handcuff gays who show affection to their partners. I have a lot of gay friends who diligently pay their taxes. They have utmost respect for the law and uphold the constitution. We have many pride parades in the States that attempts to showcase the lofty ideals of the gay population. But when the laws in Muslim countries discriminate against homosexuals, then they are unfair and inhumane. In the U.S., we even have laws against the unethical treatment of animals. We are all sentient beings able to feel and perceive. We should be able to enjoy life according to our sensory perception. We just cannot sulk in one corner and watch people go by. We ought to partake in the merriment, slacken off our inhibitions and be one with the crowd."

Fatima shook her head meaning that she was not in agreement with Linda. Her jaw dropped and was taken aback by what she heard. «I am not aware of the restrictions imposed on homosexuals in Muslim countries. I have never even met a Muslim who was a homosexual. Same-sex preference is an aberration of human behaviour that we don›t tolerate. It runs counter to the teaching of Islam. If you are a homosexual, please don›t come to our country. Don›t go about flaunting your effeminate mannerisms because it is not the true nature of man. A man is supposed to be full of vim and vigor, ready to go to battle to slay the infidels. Everyone who is not Muslim is a barbarian who deserves to be lynched.

Democracy is slowly gaining ground in Muslim countries. We have deposed long time Egyptian ruler Hosni Mubarak. We have banished into exile the despot of Tunisia who was siphoning off the government coffers. And we have unseated Algeria's decades-old president Bouteflicka who didn't want to give up power despite his age. The Muslim population has overthrown dictatorships through street protests and mass demonstrations. Muslims are freedom-loving people who abhor one-man rule. They don't deserve shabby treatment by westerners because they have proven to all that they are patriotic and love their country. We just don't want your system of loose morals spilling into our territory. Legalizing homosexuality is a deterioration of the core values of society. Homosexuals practice perverted sex that destroys the very fabric of the family. Men should couple up only with women. We live in a patriarchal society where the man is the breadwinner and the backbone of the family. Men play a crucial role in the development of the family. The role of women is secondary, relegated to the sidelines, doing household chores and caring for the children. The woman should support the man in all his endeavours. She should not be loud and brash but subdued and demure. This the only way you'll achieve harmony."

Jonas came and brought his brother Francisco with him who sought help for his addiction to alcohol. Since Jonas and Elsa already knew one another, there was no need for an introduction.

Jonas said, «How are you Elsa? How are you coping with the untimely death of William?»

Elsa replied, «I›ve been having nightmares and my blood curdles just thinking about it. Sometimes I lie awake at night thinking if I could›ve done something to prevent this horrible tragedy from occurring. I had bad vibes about the guy. One time I locked him out of the house but he began shouting invectives and giving me the finger. William was naive enough to let him in. He gave me a cold stare as if I were a mere househelp ready to be removed. But few people knew that I really cared about William, willing to do his bidding. I hardly expected the guy to bludgeon William to death because I was confident that he would choose his friends wisely. God! I don't even know the assassin's name.»

Jonas said these words to console Elsa, «Don›t feel bad Elsa. It was not your fault. Nobody saw it coming. I saw the guy too and sidled up to William to whisper unsavory comments about me. By just looking at him, I knew my days with William were numbered.

He was possessive of William, always yearning to be the center of attention. In one unguarded moment, I saw both of them hugging one another and William lustfully wanted to touch his body. They groped each other in one dark corner while I just gave a blind eye to what they were doing. William probably picked up the guy in a bar or a strip joint and offered him a place to stay in exchange for sexual favors. At his age, I never thought William would be pumping so much testosterone into his system. The man was old enough to be my father. Instead of enjoying his retirement, he chose to spend it with the dregs of society."

Jonas stepped aside and introduced his brother Francisco to the crowd now gathered. Francisco spoke, «You might not know the reason for my being here. I am just wondering whether a prayer group can reduce my dependence on alcohol. My life has been a mess because I even have bottles of whiskey stashed in my closet. Most of the time I am disoriented due to a hangover that enervates my whole body. I feel a numbness because of the debilitating effects of alcohol and I am powerless to lessen my daily intake of booze. I used to see a psychiatrist but to no avail. I still can finish a bottle of liquor a day even if I know that it makes me sluggish and ill-tempered. I know I can›t do this alone.

I need the help of ministers who will come to my aid so I can break this vicious habit. It is making me useless and has impaired my ability to think and act accordingly."

Sister Claire volunteered these words of solace. «We will pray to God that you will be able to surmount the difficult situation you›re in. May you have the strength to conquer your desire for another drink. From within these four walls, you will find support from loving people who will guide you every step of the say. A lot of people with problems have come to this ministry to seek a solution. And they were not disappointed. Aside from this group, you can head out to a center for disintoxication so you can find medical assistance for rehabilitation. You must take medication to lessen your craving for a drink. Moodiness, irregular sleeping hours and loss of appetite are but a few symptoms of alcoholism. I know you can survive this hurdle. I know of a guy who attended our group meeting and had a similar problem like yours. After a few sessions and regular visits to the rehab, he's been dry ever since. Miracles happen and there is nothing that God cannot do."

Francisco thanked Sister Claire for the words of support. His breath smelled of alcohol but he was sober enough to join the others in prayer. Some of the effects of alcoholism were hallucinations and mental torment and these were all just figments of the imagination. He wanted to put a stop to all this by giving up the bottle.

Next up was Laurie Wood. An ageing actress who during her heyday was an epitome of glamour on the silver screen. She was well past her prime and now had wrinkles and crows feet at the corner of her eyes to show to the public. She was the star of several blockbuster movies and wore costumes that are on display at the wax museum. She was novminated several times for a film award and garnered a statuette on one of her performances. She was also recognized for a lifetime achievement award by the National Film Board. She still had movie offers but they were few and far between. Directors cast her in roles that were right for her age. She used to play lead roles but due to her age, she only now played supporting roles. One time she played a supporting role in a science fiction movie but due to time constraints, portions of her scenes were cut out by the editing team. Due to dwindling movie offers, she could no longer afford her extravagant lifestyle. She was living beyond her means and incurred a lot of debt Her screen partners left her for younger film actresses who were neophytes in the business. She was a screen siren before and wore skimpy outfits in some of her films. She wore dark glasses and a bandana to cover her graying hair. She was practically retired now and offered these words of advice to beginners.

"Never reject a film offer because it may be your last. You need exposure so your face will be etched in their memory. You can make commercial endorsements to enhance your career and promote a product because of its viable ingredients. Never bare too much skin because it can hamper your profession in the long run. Once the mystery of your body is unraveled, there'll be nothing left to show. Always yearn to do wholesome movies because people of all ages will idolize you and you will become a household name. Avoid the sunlight because it hastens the ageing process. I learned too late and now that I am a wrinkled prune, I can no longer retrieve my lost youth. Drink vitamin supplements to avoid memory loss. You'll need a sharp mind when you deliver those lines in front of a camera. Try to learn many foreign languages with the right pronounciation of words. This will widen the scope of your acting skills and make you a more versatile performer. Go to a drama school so you can hone your craft. Go to a reputed dermatologist for ultimate skin care. Once you notice any creases on your face, have some collagen injections to retain that vibrant, youthful look. Set aside money for surgical intervention. As time progresses, the advancement of age will its toll on your body.

Do regular exercise so you can melt away the flabs and cellulites that accumulate in yiour belly and thighs. I give you these lessons so you will last long in your chosen field."

Margaret went out in front and escorted Laurie to her seat. She said, «Thank you so much for taking the time to talk to the crowd here gathered. I am sure we picked up some valuable pointers from your discourse. Appearance is indeed important for someone who deals with the public. Physical beauty is definitely an asset to get ahead with life. But those of us who are not endowed with such beautiful exterior can lay claim to the saving power of God.»

Linda commented, «I have what it takes to be a film star. A comely face, a svelte figure and luscious blonde hair. If I were an actress, I›d undress easily in front of camera crews. You have to be daring and do those bold roles while you›re young. Youth is a passing thing and crowds will line up to see your movie if you uncover the hidden secrets of your body. What good will it do to wrap your breasts with layers of clothing? I will do exactly the opposite of what Laurie has just said. I will bare it all for the people to feast their eyes on me.»

Laurie warned Linda. «You›ll be a has-been in no time. You should leave the audience wanting more. Once people have seen you naked, it›ll be hard to cast you in roles that are for general patronage. Don›t do pornographic movies because you›ll suffer a stigma.»

Next up was Janet Serrano. She was the daughter of a former president who was swept into power during a popular uprising against a dictator who ruled the country with an iron fist. The dictator was sent into exile while demonstrators filled the streets bearing placards, shouting slogans and arm-to-arm combat that galvanized opposition parties to form a united front. There was widespread discontent over the corrupt practices of the dictator and the luxurious homes that he owned overseas were sequestered by the government in an effort to crackdown on his ill-gotten wealth. Janet mobilized forces at the grassroots level to fight dishonesty in municipal and national politics and resotre integrity in the service of the government. A bodyguard was stationed outside the door.

She began, «The life of a daughter of the president is no easy task. You have to be accountable for every bad thing that happens in the country especially if the economy takes a turn for the worse. In the case of a terrorist attack you have to assure the public›s safety by increasing security personnel. You have to conduct press briefings where reporters scrutinize your every move. Even your private life is not spared criticism by movie scribes.»

Janet was recently the subject of a scathing news article citing her as the cause of the break up between a comedian and a well-known actress. Janet and the actress had a confrontation in a hotel lobby where the actress accused her as the reason for her husband's infidelity. They called each other names and the comedian hired a top lawyer to finalize claims of a fast and up-ended divorce. It was such a huge story that the airwaves were filled with differing versions of the event. Everyone was practically talking about the same subject matter exploring the different angles of the celebrity scoop. Janet suffered a setback in popularity as her name got tangled in a love triangle that few knew the eventual outcome. Pundits wondered why a bigtime actress and TV host like Janet would go out with a married actor while there were so many eligible bachelors out there willing to take her as a bride. Pairing up with a celebrity like Janet would propel the careers of aspiring politicians to greater heights because she was much loved by the public. She had such a clout with her legions of fans that people flocked to see her movies. She was the darling of the press and gave interviews left and right to various media outlets. Her stage shows with her screen partner were fully booked as all tickets were sold out. She toured America with her acting troupe that she won accolades from review boards and briskly sold tickets at venues like Caesar's palace in Las Vegas. She really didn't like politics preferring instead to bask in the success of her movies. It was her brother who continued with the legacy of his father, earning the nomination of a political party and eventually winning the office of the president. But all did not bode well for Janet as her relationship with the comedian soured. He allegedly poked a gun on her warning not to meddle in his love affairs. The incident so shook the country that soon tabloids were scrambling to get the latest news tidbits.

Janet resumed to talk. «I am distraught over my break up with Reginald King (the comedian in question). I thought I had met the man of my dreams but he turned out to be a philanderer with a nagging wife and many children born out of wedlock. It was a harrowing experience for me to undergo such a violent moment. I never thought he›d threaten me while I just gently chided him for being unfaithful.»

Sister Claire came to the assistance of Janet. «We›ll find you another man who›ll be on the same level as you. This time a man with no strings attached and from a noble lineage. Your union will be blessed by the church and you will bring forth children who will be heirs to a politcal dynasty."

Going back to Fatima, several people in the chamber asked her if she experienced any untoward incident due to her outward Muslim appearance. She stated that several times in the course of her life here, she was told by unruly young men to take off her hijab and go back to her country. She promptly went to the local authorities who reported it as a hate crime. But she'll never pack her bags and leave because she had found a home here and didn't hinder her from going to the mosque to worship. She held the view that the majority of the population were tolerant and respectful of religious differences. The new law, however, that bans ostentatious display of religious symbols by persons in professions of authority like judges, teachers and police officers was unjust. To reflect the cultural diversity of the country, people should be allowed to dress as they please. It is a violation of the constitutional right that guarantees freedom of expression for all regardless of one's religion, ethnicity or sexual orientation. If a man decides to grow his hair, put on make up and wear dresses, he should not be subject to ridicule because that's his prerogative. We must not deprive them of the liberty to be what they want to be. When the bill of secularism passed in the National Assembly, they took out the crucifix from the chamber signifying their intent to show religious neutrality.

There will be a separation of church and state that will greatly diminish the power of religion in political affairs. No more censorship of movies, only a classification board that will determine if a movie is fit for all ages. No more high ranking clergy who will join political rallies as they will be discouraged from making endorsements. No more priests occupying positions in the government as they will be demoted to the status of observer. A priest once ran a political campaign to serve as a municipal councillor. Even if he won, he will be asked to step down from his position to comply with the new law. Not long after, protestors marched through the streets demanding the abrogation of the secularism bill calling it discriminatory and unjust. It targets religious minorities who have noticed an increase in harassment and racial prejudice. Massacres of Muslims in mosques in Christchurch and Quebec city has only aggravated the situation. Muslim worshippers have to look over their shoulder to make sure that the man next to them is not armed with a submachine gun. Times of uncertainty where we all have to be vigilant about the people around us. We all have to be wary about who is entering the mosque, church or synagogue. They have to be stripsearched for the possibility of carrying firearms. This is no time to be complacent.

Fatima expressed dissatisfaction over the complaints of many residents of a borough over the move to transform a vacant plot of land into a burial site for deceased members of the Muslim community. She said that Muslims deserved a resting place where they can perform their own brand of funeral rites.

Elsa reacted, «What difference does it make? We all bury the dead the same way. Dig a trench six feet under the ground and lower the coffin to the sweet smelling earth in the hopes that the soul would be transported to God›s presence. Like Muslims, we pray for the eternal repose of the soul and ask for their intercession to grant us favors. The only difference are the tombstones. Instead of a cross, you have a crescent. But surely they can lie side by side.»

Fatima answered, «There is a big difference between a Muslim funeral rite and Catholic rituals. We invoke the name of Allah citing verses in the Koran while you pray to graven images of saints who are actually deceased people. You should pray only to Allah who is the source of happiness.»

Sister Claire recapped their conversation. «Whoever you are, you›re destined for an afterlife with God. What matters is that we do good deeds to our fellowman which is appealing to God. Our body decays but our soul lives on. The body returns to dust while we should utter blessings for the dearly departed.»

Next up was retired constable Peter Trent. He was an indomitable figure in the police force who showed no restraint when it came to the apprehension of criminals. He brokered a peace agreement between rival street gangs detaining their leaders and charging them with drug trafficking and abduction of minors who were forced into juvenile prostitution. The gang members bore distinctive tattoos on their chests and biceps to signify their connection with a specific group. He was awarded a medal of freedom by the government which recognized his herculean efforts at wiping away organized crime. Uncer the aegis of his police force, the crime rate went down as checkpoints were installed in many parts of the city to stop the spread of thuggery, automobile theft and petty crimes. There was a clampdown on graft and corruption as his department collaborated with the ombudsman to bring to justice erring government officials. The missing children's network got a boost from his participation as he combed through the hillsides and wide areas of the city and found a few kidnapped children who were later reunited with their families. He established a toll free hotline that gathered tips from the general public to delve into unsolved criminal cases and act on leads that would direct them to the hideout of missing persons. He was against the legalization of prostitution arguing that the sex trade would put vulnerable women at risk. There were still many wanted criminals who were at large. He posted their pictures in the bureau's website asking for the cooperation of the public leading to the arrest and capture of said criminals. Their crimes ranged from fraud, underground commerce of crack and cocaine and the recruitment of women for purposes of sex slavery. One time there was a man who inadvertently left his credit card at the cash register. The cashier figured out the PIN number and started making illegal purchases with the card. The police traced the illegal activity to the store and subsequently the culprit was caught, imprisoned and told to pay for damages. Another time a woman with a baby carriage shoplifted several clothing items from a store stuffing them in the stroller. She was eventually released after she surrendered the loot and also because of her precarious situation. His police division also took charge of the homeless finding them temporary shelter so they don't shiver in the cold. Other times there were drug addicts dying of an overdose in the streets with their bodies splayed on the ground. They were promptly loaded into the ambulance where they received excellent care by medical personnel As for missing children, he'd have their photos published on cartons of milk so the public would better recognize them.

Retired constable Peter Trent spoke. «I have been with the police force for over forty years and never have I encountered such a heartwarming congregation showing care and concern for one another. If only the rest of the population would show the same level of interest in the well-being of their fellow citizens then we wouldn›t have such a daunting task ahead of us.»

Margaret stepped in and spoke these words, «You are very welcome to join this prayer group. The people here are patient and accomodating. The people here don't find fault with one another and are very understanding. You are an instrument of God solving crimes, punishing those who violate the law and keeping peace and order in the country. A person of your stature will be a driving force for the church to act in accordance with the law."

Constable Trent answered, «I am glad that I am well received by the church. The church is a valuable ally in our campaign to tackle those who subvert the law. I am impressed by your willingness to cooperate with law enforcement officers and only hope for a fruitful partnership.»

During the summer months when the temperature often exceeds 35 degrees celsius it is important to keep yourself hydrated by drinking plenty of water and staying under the shade. Avoid doing physical exercise like jogging or lifting weights as this can increase body temperature and lead to dizziness and fainting spells. The medical division is on the lookout for vulnerable people especially the elderly, those who suffer from chronic heart disease and young infants who may not be used to the sweltering heat. Encourage people to stay indoors and not to exert too much effort in physical activity. Go to a place where there are air conditioners in order to freshen up and remain invigorated. During this time you will often see people jauntily bathing in water fountains, wading their feet in the cool stream or eating ice cream in order to fight the heat. Men take off their shirts while women are clad in scanty bathing suits to better adjust to the heat. Make sure your dogs are fed well with gallons of water so they don't die of exhaustion. Never walk your dog under direct sunshine because they can burn their paws from the hot pavement. Try not to venture outside in the noonday sun preferring instead to walk in the late afternoon. Horses have collapsed due to the extreme heat prompting city officials to ban horse-drawn carriages. Some parades and sporting events have been cancelled because of the scorching heat. The marathaon that draws many onlookers to its location has been postponed to a later date due to the unseasonably hot weather. If you have plants in clay pots, bring them in so the leaves don't wither from too much sun. Douse your dogs and horses with buckets of water so they don't break down in the intense heat. During a sunny and hot day, take advantage of the situation by drying out your ckothes in a clothesline. You can also expose your mattress and blankets in the noonday sun to sterilize them and kill the lice and bed bugs that may be present. Open your windows to let the air in. Make sure that your room is well ventilated so you don't suffocate and sweat inside. Since the ground is parched and arid. never light a bonfire because it can get out of control and raze the entire neighborhood. If you have to go outside, bring a black umbrella to shield yourself from the dangerous ultraviolet rays.

In an apartment guilding, membeers of the paramedic team are going door to door to make sure that the tenants do not suffer from the heat. They install airconditioning units to rooms that do not have adquate ventilation. The team also makes sure that the refrigerators are working so they can supply the occupants with refreshments and cold drinks. Outdoor swimming pools are teeming with people at this time of the year. There has to be a lifeguard stationed there so nobody will drown. Bathing in rivers is strongly discouraged because you might get swept away by the strong current. When swimming at a beach, make sure you swim up to the recommended distance or within sight of the lifeguard to avoid deadly encounters with sharks and manta rays. When sunbathing in a beach, always bring a bottle of suntan lotion to avoid sunburns and melanoma of the skin. Due to the overexposure to the sun, you may experience redness and swelling of the skin. If symptoms persist, consult a physician.

Even Laurie Wood, the sexagenarian, was feeling a bit dizzy due to the intense heat outside. But Margaret brought her a glass of water with ice cubes to drink and she began to feel refreshed. People her age are sensitive to rising temperatures and need constant care and attention. After responding well to the refreshment, she signified her intent to stay until the conclusion of the prayer meeting. The weather forecast called for a light wind from the south bringing in hot and humid air to the city. It is important to plant trees because they absorb the dangerous gases that come from trucks, buses and cars. Francisco was also feeling tipsy because of his perennial probelm with alcohol but after a drink of cold water, he sobered up.

Elsa was sitting in a corner reminiscing about her trip to Vancouver which William, her employer, paid for. It was in January when they went, the middle of winter and there were copious amounts of snow that fell from the sky. There were children playing ice hockey on a dead end street complete with a goalie and had hockey sticks to hit the puck. Their skates made a grating sound as there was friction with the sleet of ice that covered the pavement. Hocky was the national past time so it was common to see this sport being practiced during winter. She marveled at the sight of the Rockies, Western Canada's chain of mountains, with its snowcapped mountains and dense arboreal forest. The sunlight could not even peek through the canopy of trees where bears thrived on the ground hibernating in the cold. She tried her hand on skiing as she slid down the mountain slope. Luckily she didn't hit any tree but just tumbled in the snow. There were some intrepid adventurers who rode the bobsleigh through the snow. They were adept at winter sports tobogganing downhill at the mountain side. Elsa was well-equipped for the winter. She wore leather gloves with a woolen sweater and a goose down jacket. She wore a thick scarf around her neck and a knitted cap that covered her ears from the cold. She also wore boots that were lined with a thick fabric to keep her toes warm.

She met an Asian caregiver who was in a difficult situation. She was threatened with deportation due to the unexplained death of an elderly woman in an old age home. Her name was Sylvia Custodio and she was appealing her case through the work of her lawyers. She was suspected of administering an overdose of medication since she had daily access to the bedside of the victim. Elsa visited Sylvia several times in the detention center to give her moral support and promised to give her legal assistance through different channels of the government. Sylvia was Elsa's compatriot who had strong ties and many relatives in their country of origin. Elsa contacted a lawyer to act on the dismissal of the case due to a lack of evidence. It was important that Sylvia stays in Canada because she was just weeks away in achieving her landed immigrant status. Aside from that, she was the sole provider for her family. She had plans of petitioning her entire family to come work in Canada.

William introduced Elsa to a member of the academe now living in Vancouver. His name was Steven Camacho who was living in a three bedroom apartment in a posh area of the city. Steven ran a magazine that published articles concerning hispanic culture. William was a prolific writer for the magazine. Steven showed them the sights and sounds of the city. He brought them to watch a musical presentation at the Queen Elizabeth theater. Elsa thoroughly enjoyed it. The final act made Elsa cry and she reached for the handkerchief of William to wipe away her tears.

But Elsa would not shed a tear for William›s assassin whose image continued to haunt her. Where could the murderer be? There was a nationwide manhunt and it was very difficult to elude arrest. Did he find another benefactor who was gullible enought to give him shelter? How long before another murder takes place and shatters the fragile peace of the neighborhood? No one can sleep well at night knowing that a dangerous criminal is no the loose. But with the scant amount of information relating to the identity of the suspect, it was hard to pin him down. No finger prints, no pictures, just an artist's sketch based on the tenuous recollection of a woman in the state of shock. She was in her home turf now but she felt a longing to be in Vancouver. It would not be long before she started the paperwork to immigrate as a retiree.

Next up at the podium was Galina Ivanovych. She was a Russian opera singer who sang at the Covent Garden, England. She specialized in the operas of Verdi and Puccini. She also sang in her native russian in the operas of Tchaikovsky most notably in the Queen of Spades and Eugene Onegin. She was a lyric soprano who could surpass two and a half octaves in singing. She was impressed by the choir at the church because they had loud and clear voices singing the hymns in a forceful manner. She made her debut at the stage when an Italian singer became indisposed due to a cold. It was in the opera Tosca and her performance was widely acclaimed earning several curtain calls from the audience. She traveled transatlantic to sing in New York city. After a week of publicity, tickets to her stage performance was sold out. She had a solo number at the church singing Ave Maria during a Christmass mass to a packed audience. She was accompanied by the organ and the number was flawlessly executed. There was thunderous applause after the rendition and the crowd cried for an encore. There was an unforgettable moment during a stage performance of Tosca shen she jumps from the parapet to escape the local authorities. She was extra nervous that night and asked that they double the number of mattresses at the bottom of the stage.

When she jumped, she sprung back up eliciting laughter from the audience. Another time she could not forget was during a production of La Boheme when her wig caught fire from a lit candle. There was pandemonium on the stage as crews started dousing the flames with buckets of water. The curtains went down and a twenty minute intermission was called to rectify the situation and assess the damage. When it was confirmed that Galina had not suffered any injuries, the show resumed.

Galina especially had a liking for two singers in the choir who showed great potential. One was tenor Joel Lieberman whose stentorian voice had a magnificent ring to it. The other was Ana Schwartz. Her voice spanned three octaves and was capable of singing topmost notes. Galina was convinced that she was a coloratura most suited in the operas of Bellini and Donizetti. Galina encouraged the two singers to audition for the new season of the opera company. She offered them free vocal instruction so that they could familiarize themselves with operatic roles.

Galina would spend her time beside the piano doing solfeggio exercises and playing operatic tunes which she would sing along with. She had this advice for singers. Refrain from eating ice cream because this incites the production of mucus and phlegm which coats the vocal chords and is an obstacle to singing clearly. Instead, you should drink citric juices which keeps away colds and laryngitis. Never sleep in an area where there is a cold draught of wind. This could lead to sinusitis, pneumonia and migraine headaches and can affect your performance. Don't scream or talk too much before a performance because this could strain your vocal chords. Avoid second hand smoke because this can lead to a coughing fit and fill your lungs with noxious gases. Cigarette smoke contains many carcinogenic elements and it's best to keep away from it so your lungs will be infused with fresh oxygen. Get adequate sleep so your voice will be in tiptop shape. Vocalize daily, going up and down the musical scale to train the sonority and flexibility of your voice.

Her cellphone rang. It was her agent who told her to fly to London within a week to substitute for an ailing soprano. It was for the title role of La Gioconda, an opera she had never sang before. A new production was in place and rehearsals were under way. She would share topbilling with a stellar cast who all had arias to sing. She would stick around for the prayer meeting but would have to pack her bags in haste and head for the airport as soon as possible. She was so in demand and had so many engagements to fulfill.

Elsa was discussing the rudiments of the case with Constable Peter Trent. Constable Trent said he was familiar with the case because it grubbed the headlines and was broadcast in the daily newscast. He averred that he wanted to reinstate the death penalty for crimes such as rape, murder and the abduction of children. But to have the capital punishment passed into law, they would need a two thirds majority of the House who will vote in favor of the bill. The death penalty was repealed after the wrongful convictions of several high profile cases where the crime could not be proven without a shadow of a doubt. Suspects are languishing in jail awaiting trial for their cases. Convicted crimininals on death row have earned a reprieve for their punishment commuting their sentences to life imprisonment. A less severe form of punishment was in order for hardcore criminals who volunteered to participate in a rehabilitation program. Persons convicted of minor crimes like shoplifting, vandalism and the illegal possession of small quantities of drugs were to undergo psychiatric evaluation and a general health check up before being released in a halfway house en route to the eventual integration with society. Many would undergo training so they can acquire skills necessary to obtain employment. Added measures were in place at airports increasing security personnel so they can effectively identify and arrest suspects before they board a plane. Once a suspect has slipped through security and traveled abroad, it will be hard to repatriate him because the country doesn't have an extradition treaty with many countries. Aside from customs inspectors and x-ray machines, sniffer dogs were on standby alert to detect if illegal drugs were hidden in luggages or carry-on baggages. It was not long ago when a Chinese national was arrested for illegal possession of 50 kilograms of cocaine stuffed in her suitcase. She was subsequently charged by the regional trial court and is awaiting her hearing.

In the coastal city, port authorities uncovered an illegal shipment of untaxed and undeclared tobacco that had a street value of two million dollars destined for the consumption of the local population. An American this time was behind the attempt to smuggle tobacco and was sent to an immigration detention facility awaiting deportation. He was also ordered to pay a fine of a half a million dollars in unpaid taxes. Other items seized by the port authority were luxury cars, trademark handbags and fake watches that would have easily circulated in the city with no one knowing where they came from. Cruise ships would often dock at the harbor with passengers disembarking to see the scenic spots in the country. While no one was looking, clandestine passengers would surreptitiously board the vessel in search of a new country. It is not known whether there were any criminals among these stowaways. There was a move to update the record keeping division of the statistics office. A number would be assigned to every citizen with the data collected under his file. Finger prints, color of eyes and employment earnings will be stored in his dossier. The state will force every citizen to fill out a census form so they can revise their records. Citizens would be required to fill out a ten page questionnaire on matters concerning languages spoken, employment history, age and gender. The information gathered will be kept confidential unless asked by the bureau of immigration and the police force to release vital details.

They already found DNA material from the sample of semen found in the bedsheet at William›s house. All they need to do now is to find a match. But Elsa wondered what if the suspect had already left the country. Constable Trent responded that the chances of him going abroad are slim taking into account that he had no passport, no birth certificate or other pertinent documents. Dry, encrusted semen found at the bed would serve as incontrovertible proof of the suspect›s complicity in the crime.

Next up was Frederic Villeneuve. He was a telemarketeer who sold paper rolls, ink cartridges and directory listings. Materials for the cash register and advertisement to enhance the business. The rules of the job were simple. Sell at least three items at three hundred dollars each to fill your quota. The more sales you make, the more commission you earn. The business was called Infotel and it was owned by a pair of enterprising brothers. Frederic filled his quota every week and even surpassed the basic requirement. He spoke English eloquently and delivered his lines with finesse and complete composure. Each desk was equipped with a phone and each caller was given a script which they would say to the customer. There were many desks in the call center and business was running smoothly. Many callers had a glib tongue engaging the customer in a long winded conversation. The caller would talk to the cutomer about many things, asking about their health or how their business was doing. As a rule, they only called businesses because the products involved here were for commercial purposes. Frederic was employed in another line of work before but didn't like it because it was too strenuous. He worked for a burger joint and had to mop the floor, clean the trays, operate the dishwasher and make a sandwich per minute After a few months on the job, he gave up and quit. He preferred tlemarketing because he didn't have to exert any physical effort. He'd sit back in his desk, get comfortable in his chair and dial the number. The crux of the matter was how to convince the customer that he needed the products for his business. It always pays to be friendly, find something in common and give a few tips so that their business will grow. One time Frederic came across a customer who said that all she got was junk mail after being listed in the company directory. Frederic argued that her business would pick up especially during the holiday season and that all she needed to do was be patient. Hundreds of customers can attest to the fact that because of the directory listing, their business grew to make a huge profit. She also confided to Frederic about her family problems. Her son was getting failing grades at school and her daughter was reprimanded for wearing too revealing dresses on campus. After a lengthy conversation, Frederic advised her to have a heartfelt conversation with her children. The call ended and a transaction was completed. The day after, the sale went through with the customer signifying her intent to purchase the products.

It was a 9 to 5 job with no problems in looking for customers. Since their time zone was Eastern Standard time, they could practically call the whole continent. Calling the Pacific states would come later in the afternoon because of the time difference. Most of their customers lived in the United States so there was no language barrier, no hindrance of schedules and only a top currency to earn. Many nationalities worked at the call center. Some top telemarketeers were nationals from the Indian subcontinent. They were fluent in English and delivered their lines in an effortless manner. Physical appearance wasn't really important in this kind of a job since it was the tone of voice and the diction that mattered. One caller was discharged from her employment because her speech was heavily accented. The customers simply could not comprehend what she was saying. She came from the Caribbean and spoke slang most of the time. One customer remarked about the French accent of Frederic. She complimented him about his peculiar way of speaking. It differed markedly from American pronounciation which was uncommon and distinctive. He would regale the listener with stories about his life in France. The exquisite cuisine, the breathtaking landmarks and the expertly sewn dresses of top French couturiers. Of course, not everyone comes from a rich cultural background as Frederic which is why he's a very talented telemarketeer.

Next up was business owner Judith Kramer who owned a restaurant at Audubon Avenue. Her restaurant specialized in Italian dishes like lasagna, ravioli, pizza and spaghetti. The dining area was large with a sizable seating capacity of fifteen talbes. They had a bar that served beer and other carbonated beverages. Customers were told to wait at the foyer until they could be seated. There was usually a line up and customers were told to come back in an hour so they could have a table. Judith employed a lot of waiters who were dressed in black pants and white long sleeved shirts. One such waitress was Janice Ford who was a student in art history at the Wheaton University. She worked part time and had a lucky encounter with a client who tipped her two hundred dollars for excellent service. She almost always served customers who gave generous tips. One time she came to work wearing high heeled shoes. Her feet started to get tired and asked Judith if she could lend her flat heeled shoes. Luckily, there were slippers in the corner and Judith handed them to her. You can't last the day if you wear stiletto heels going from table to table. Judith was criticized for her hiring practices. She employed only Mediterranean looking waiters and waitresses to give the ambiance a festive Italian flavor. Blacks and other people of color were relegated to the back working as dishwashers, janitors and busboys. She vehemently denied she was a racist arguing that an agreeable appearance was necessary to entice the customers to come in. She wanted to run a profitable business and not a shelter for the homeless. Frederic sat beside Judith and asked her if she was interested in purchasing materials for the business. She replied in the affirmative and publicly stated that she was exploring the possibility of expanding her business to other parts of the city. Her chefs came direct from Italy and were well trained to cook up the specialties. She had various kinds of pizza. A lot people loved her pizza with pepperoni, anchovies, green pepper and mushrooms. Her pizza had a thin crust with a generous layer of mozzarella cheeze. She had two wooden ovens that baked the pizza in three hundred fifty degree heat. She had already been to Italy where she studied the different culinary techniques of Italian gastronomy. She imported the best Italian wine distilled from grapes grown at the Po river valley and near lake Cuomo. The temperate climate was ideal for growing grapes and the fruit was ripened to perfection. Her full red tomatoes from which she made her tomato sauce came from the Napa valley in California. They weren't flaccid or soft but were firm and juicy just ripe for the picking.

She ordered crates of tomato which she stored in a huge refrigerator. She only bought the best pasta from reputed Italian specialty outlets. The dough they made themselves from the finest ingredients available in the market. She told Margaret that she would like to adveritse her restaurant in the parish bulletin. There were thirty per cent discounts for students and seniors every Wednesday. They had to bring a piece of identification to show proof of age and connection with the school. Many customers who couldn't find a seat ordered their food at the take out counter. Needless to say, the cash register was always ringing as the restaurant was swamped with orders. The restaurant got excellent grades from food inspectors who came to examine the cleanliness of the place and the freshness of food. The restaurant got good ratings from culinary experts wjho came to sample the food. It was highly recommended for those who want to savor Italian cuisine. There was piped in music from contemporary Italian singers. Also heard in full stereo were excerpts from Italian operas. There were oil paintings on the wall from several renowned Italian artists. Eating at the restaurant was an enriching experience that was both unforgettable and delightful.

Laurie Wood and Galina Ivanovych were comparing notes about their lustrous careers. One was already in decline while the other was reaping rave reviews for her electrifying performance on stage. Galina won the prestigious award from the roster of the Metropolitan opera performers as most promising upcoming singer to ever emerge in the new millenium. It was equivalent to the statuette won by Laurie Wood for her performance in the blockbuster movie "The woman has two faces". The story is about a woman who gets widowed early and gets a chance to prove her worth by pursuing a career in the fashion business. She designs clothes and wins the approval of critics, making a curtsey at the catwalk surround by a bevy of slender models. The work of fiction wasn't far from reality as Laurie was named one of the most elegant women in the country. The dresses she wore on screen were fabricated from the best textiles made by top designers. When she made her entrance in a movie, it was always with bated breath that the audience waited for her to appear. The same was for Galina who wore costumes that were appropriate for the period in which the stage was set. One time she wore flowing robes and an ornate headgear for her performance in Turandot. It was well received by the audience who were moved by her poignant rendition of a turn of the century princess. Her robe had sequins and imitation pearls which glistened in the stage lighting. While Galina would sing almost always in Italian, Laurie would deliver her lines in English. But the movies of Laurie were dubbed in several European languages so that the audience could follow the plot. There were also English subtitles to the operas performed by Galina so that the spectators could understand what was being sung. Singing was more physically taxing than merely saying the lines because it involved the whole range of the voice. In the opera Turandot, for example, the role calls for a dramatic soprano who could sing and be audible inspite of a loud orchestra. Galina could easily manage this feat soaring above the sound of drums and cymbals that gave the opera a majestic atmosphere. Physical exercise was strongly encouraged to better handle jitters or stage fright. There will be better contraction of stomach muscles that will help in the movement of the diaphragm. Breathing sufficient oxygen is key to sustaining vocal strength and singing those difficult passages in a musical score. Coping with a busy schedule is what takes most of the time of Galina. Rehearsals were held almost everyday so that the production will run smoothly.

The members of the orchestra were tuning their instruments to achieve perfect pitch. Violinists only played a Stradivarius to perform music of excellent quality. The kinks in the production were ironed out like lighting defects or ill-conceived stage property. Galina was fully booked for the next two years and had no time to entertain suitors. She had white skin, rosy lips and an aquiline nose that was a reflection of her Slavic bloodline. As for Laurie Wood, she was an American with a mixing of native American heritage. Galina lived in a stately home in Westford Avenue in the company of two poodles. She had a maidservant who took care of her needs. Life of an upcoming singer wasn't easy because of her hectic schedule. She would shuttle from country to country unpacking her clothes from her suitcase and living in hotels most of the time. On the contrary, the life of Laurie was more laid back having practically retired from the movies. The moment Galina would step out of the plane, she'd have to meet the production team for some costume fitting. Rehearsals would commence in the afternoon that would give her time to shake off the jetlag due to the time difference. For the production of La Gioconda, she was going to put on light make up and wear a nineteenth century Venetian dress. The opera was set in Italy. Such was the busy schedule of Galina and she was grateful for the many opportunities that life has to offer.

Laurie Wood and Galina Ivanovych were exchanging pleasantries. Laurie asked her a question. "What preparations have you been making to tackle your new role at Covent Garden? Have you memorized your lines?"

Galina answered, «La Gioconda is a fairly easy role to remember. I know the opera by heart. Whenever I have time, I go see operas and how they are performed on stage. That way I have an idea on how to project my voice and move on the stage. I have to follow the cue as indicated by the composer and sing through quartets and trios. That is why we rehearse everyday so the timing is perfect. Why don›t you make the trip halfway around the world to come see me."

Laurie responded, «I›m on a tight budget. I used to be able to afford these things until I fell victim to a scam of more than a million dollars. I was romantically linked to my impresario before. He whispered sweet things to me and I trusted him. I forked out a huge sum of money to pay for our marriage plans. Once he had the money, he took off and I never heard from him again. But I'm still making money from my former movies. They've been reissued in DVD format and I collect royalties from the sale. I'm still a popular actress in showbiz and my reputation hasn't been tarnished by scandals unlike some other actresses. I just wish I come across a good role at my age that will serve as the crowning achievement of my long career."

Galina added these lines, «You›re lucky you lasted this long. I›m taking care of my voice so I can last until retirement age. I haven›t made up my mind yet on whether I should sing Wagnerian roles. The roles ask for a dramatic soprano who can sing through a thirty two piece orchestra. I certainly have the ability to sing these roles but don›t know whether it›s going to take a toll on my voice. I have to be careful when choosing roles. It's still early in my career and I have a lot of studying to do. I have to pore through the librettos and memorize the lines. Anyway, in case you forget your lines, there's always a stage prompter who is hidden from view. He coaches you on the next lines that you'll sing."

Laurie inserted a remark. «I never had problems remembering my lines. If one of the actors made a blunder, we could always call for another take. Otherwise, we›d do ad libs and the scene would pass muster by the director. Because of my age, my chances of having a plum role in a movie have whittled down to a paltry few. Anyway, the long line up of movies I made is a testament to the fact that I had such a glorious career. If they're doing a sequel on one of my movies, they're having a difficult time finding a replacement with the right chemistry and the dashing good looks. Even at my age, I don't dye my hair and have never had plastic surgery to rejuvenate my face. No tummy tuck, no breast implants and no face lift. I have aged gracefully and wouldn't want to alter the trajectory of my career. I don't want to put on too much make up and appear all dolled up like a corpse in a coffin. I just dab a little blush powder on my cheeks and a pink lipstick on my lips to get that light glow from my flawless complexion."

Galina commented, «I am impressed that at your age you still get movie offers. I hope I›ll still be able sing at your age.»

Laurie answered, «They're planning to do a movie based on the novel Madame Bovary and I am a frontrunner chosen to play the lead role. If that comes to pass, it will be my swansong before I finally bow out from the screen. They need a woman of a ripe age and with a regal bearing. I most certainly fit the description and with my experience, I can play the role convincingly. I've played the role of an aristocrat many times set in luxurious villas. It will just be another jewel in my crown."

Next up was Jeannie Anderson. She was a nurse at Lakeshore General Hospital. She was in charge of the left wing of the fourth floor, from room number 402 up to 404. She was a patient and kind nurse always on call for patients suffering from discomfort, minor aches and joint pain. She would give them shots to relieve them from the effects of dysentery, typhoid and measles. After the initial diagnosis by a competent physician, she would dispense antibiotics to stop the spread of diseases. One patient showed symptoms of diarrhea and epileptic seizures. She gave him a tranquilizer and a stool stabilizer to soothe his condition. There were several diabetics in the hospital ward and their sugar level had to be checked regularly. She gave them shots of insulin, as well as, oral medication to lower their glucose level and cautioned them to reduce their sugar intake. The only kind of sugar allowed was from fruit juices and artificial sweeteners which were used in coffee or tea. She was in no position to prescribe medicines. Only the doctor did that. She did, however, follow instructions, administering the right dosage and the time indicated on the label. For skin diseases like psoriasis and vitiligo, she would wash her hands and wear latex gloves while she applied ointment to the affected area. Usually, she would wear a mask to avoid smelling the infection.

For those suffering from wounds and lacerations, she would change the dressing daily and clean it before with an antiseptic solution. She would then cover the wound with a bandage to protect it from external elements. She would insert needles to the veins of patients to draw blood needed for exams. Through blood samples one can detect infirmities or abnormalities that affect the body. She also mounted intravenous tubes above the bed to supply medication to the body in addition to pills taken by the patient. The liquid in plastic bags were clear and colourless and used to fight infections.

With eyes downcast and a bit of shame Janet Serrano asked her what measures should she take to cure her chlamydia. Jeannie Anderson responded that chlamydia is a sexually transmitted disease and there should be an ongoing treatment to flush out the infection. One dose of penicillin that is taken orally may not be enough to treat the disease. Some sexually transmitted diseases are drug resistant so immunotherapy is required to suppress it. Chlamydia is acquired if one has many sexual partners. Janet said her boyfriend gave it to her through one of his indiscretions.

One patient had parasites in his bowels but didn't need hospitalization. He could be treated as an out-patient with a prescription of deworming medication. His sheets and pillowcases should be changed daily to halt further contamination by eggs of the parasite.

Those who suffered from vehicular accidents and were partly paralyzed were left in the emergency wing for further observation. Jeannie had worked in this section alleviating the trauma that these accident victims are going through. If the condition worsened due to a festering wound, the patient would be transferred to the intensive care unit.

There were get well cards pinned on the bulletin board for patients billeted in the hospital. They were from family and friends who wished them a speedy recovery. There were also Thank you cards from grateful patients who were cured from their illnesses. They thanked the nurses for their diligent work, undivided attention and unwavering support. Jeannie sometimes did the graveyard shift whenever there was shortage of staff. She made her rounds to see if the patients were sound asleep and supply sleeping pills to insomniacs. For those who were sore, she gave them painkillers to take them out of misery. Jeannie was a well-rounded person, energetic and dynamic. She always responded promptly to the patient›s needs. A professional who knew how to prick needles on the skin with the least irritation. If she had a premonition that something would go wrong with the patient, she would advise the relatives to prepare for the worst. Many unexpected deaths had occurred in the hospital due to a sudden complication or an incurable condition. But there was never any incidence of malpractice.

Jonas and Francisco approached the nurse Jeannie Anderson with a question to ask. After pondering on what to say, Francisco caught his breath and explained his predicament. "I'm struggling with my addiction to alcohol for a long time and wonder if there is any medicine that will lessen my urge to drink. It can't go on this way. There's gotta be a way out."

Jeannie answered, «Alcoholism is a form of mental illness and is treated with care and understanding. Unfortunately, the drugs may have an adverse effect on you when taken with alcohol. The treatment will be ineffective and will not limit your hankering for another drink. The only alternative for you is to summon up your will power and voluntarily give up drinking. You can talk it out with a group like the Alcoholics Anonymous sessions where you will encounter people with similar hang ups like yours. For recovering alcoholics we usually prescribe anti-depressants like zoloft. This is to reduce the gravity of your mood swings."

Francisco continued, «I stay awake and cry at night. My whole savings have been frittered away by my consumption of alcohol. I have tremors in my body and sometimes I shake uncontrollably. I suffer from severe convulsions due to visions of impending doom. How to stop this delirium?»

Jeannie answered, «You obviously have a nervous condition. We can help only so much but the rest is up to you. One by one your friends will desert you, if that hasn't happened already and you'll be left by your lonesome self to forage for your next meal. Witness the many homeless people living in the street. They've been rejected by their family with nowhere to go. No one can put up with an unmitigated disaster like an addiction to alcohol. Alcoholism can lead to the early onset of Alzheimer's disease. Slowly your brain cells will begin to diminish and you will start having memory lapses. You will forget more easily and you will be out of touch with reality. You will fall into a deep stupor and you will be unable to distinguish shapes and sizes. You will suffer from a mental black out due to the numbing effects of alcohol."

It was Jonas›s turn to vent his frustration with the family. He spoke to Jeannie Anderson. «For several years now, I've been having a long-standing feud with my brother. He hollers invectives at me and even threatens to do physical harm. I have problems sleeping at night due to the domestic violence and have turned to taking sedatives sometimes to allay my fears. Are there other medicines that can help me rest from the voices I hear?"

Jeannie answered, «You›re suffering from paranoid schizophrenia and need to take anti-psychotic drugs like risperdal and seroquel. If you live in an unhealthy environment, it's best to separate from the source of the stress.

You have mental anxieties that can lead to a nervous breakdown and a complete disorder of cognitive abilities. You have to identify the root cause of your tension and avoid that which is detrimental to your health. I have a question for you both. Do you have any suicidal tendencies or thoughts about harming yourself?"

Jonas was first to respond. «I know this crisis is temporary and will eventually be overcome. If we part ways then I will be able to find the peace that I seek. But until then, I have to seek counselling about the long-term effects of this turmoil.»

Francisco also replied, «If I don›t find a solution soon to my excessive drinking, I might end up in a box. Already I›ve been diagnosed with cirrhosis of the liver and suffer from jaundice due to the disproportionate amount of bile in my bloodstream. It›s good to discuss my problem out in the open so I don›t feel alone in tackling this crisis.»

Jeannie warned Francisco. «If you drink too much, you won›t be able to perform in bed. You will suffer from erectile dysfunction, unable to get it up and ejaculate. You will suffer from a low sperm count, unable to produce offspring. Your semen will be of poor consistency smelling rancid due to the thinning of the blood. The road to recovery is long and arduous but it all begins with a first step.»

Next up was George Campbell. He was a bodybuilder who won several bodybuilding competitions in the bay area due to his striking pose and excellent physique. As is customary of bodybuilders, they would apply baby oil to the entire body and flex their muscles in full view of the spectators that filled the auditorium. He had a full developed chest with hefty biceps and pectoral muscles. The judges represented a whole cross section of people that included dieticians, nutritionists, doctors, athletes and authorities on bodily functions. He would spend hours each day at the gym lifting weights, jogging on the treadmill and heaving barbells twice his scale. He was a scrawny person before and bullied at school. But he'd had enough of that and didn't want to be a sissy anymore. He started eating nutritious food in big amounts, took steroids, added weight and hired a personal trainer to supervise his phenomenal growth. He had a baritone voice that he used to drawl his words. He had a southern accent and wore a cowboy's hat most of the time. He would watch the Calgary stampede especially the rodeo event where a cowboy does his best to ride a kicking bronco. He spent a lot of his time watching a public performance featuring ranch hands riding and roping wild horses and cattle. Girls would shriek with delight at the mere sight of him as he jogged past the cypresses on the road as part of his morning exercise. He was a young man with a full mop of brown hair. He could be a model for the cover of Gentleman's Quarterly magazine or a pin up boy for a calendar. He did his stint at the catwalk modelling for a famous Italian designer. He was a favorite subject of photographers with his flat abdomen and massive muscles on the biceps and chest. He had offers to do movies but was still mulling over which role to pick. There was a role about an adventurer lost in the jungle and stumbles upon an ancient civilization. Another one was a role of a man deserted in an island left alone to fend for himself until he is rescued by what they saw was a column of smoke emanating from the ground. It was his thatched roof that got burnt and if it were not for the smoke, he wouldn't have been rescued. The film would run for ninety minutes showing him in various stages of bare-chested film tracks. Things were looking rosy in his budding career as a model and actor. His boyish good looks had a midwestern flair that was every girl's dream to have and to hold. But marriage wasn't in the cards yet as he courted many damsels and pick the fairest of them all. His was a fresh face on the market that landed on the cover of Sports Illustrated or showbiz gossip magazines. He would go on a date with young actresses carousing bars till the wee hours of the morning. There was no end to his romantic pursuits as he was virile and masculine.

Every girls's dream of being alone in an island with this hunk. He liked blonds and redheads because they had a fantastic sense of humor that tickled him pink. The dark haired variety he considered sullen and serious, no fun to be with. He had a well-balanced diet eating a generous serving of oysters to make him perform better in bed. Oysters sell for only a dollar each every Monday at Brasserie Bernard. He goes there to get his fill. He takes natural aphrodisiac in pill form to fortify his sex drive. It was important for him to have a vigorous libido so his sex partners will be satisfied even wanting more. He wasn't into buying animal parts from illegal game animals like rhino horns. If you patronized such products, you're abetting the illegal animal trade. It was widely accepted that the rhinoceros was an endangered species and should no longer be hunted by poachers. Apart from his profession as a bodybuilder, he was a firm believer in the conservation of animals. Animals should have a sanctuary where they can propagate their species. As a man, he was sent on the same mission which was to copulate with females. He spread his charm through interviews and reality TV shows. He believes that man is impinging on the territory of animals by building roads and housing subdivisions into the last remaining rain forest. He spearheads the campaign for conservation. There should be a moratorium on the killing of species that are dwindling in number.

Linda Duvalier was immediately attracted to George Campbell. She was drawn to the well-sculpted form that was the result of gruelling hours of exercise. Linda was like a swarm of maggots that was pulled towards a fresh piece of medium rare steak. She sat beside him, took a whiff of his musk scent and drooled over him showing gushing fascination. She took off her vest and said that her body temperature was beginning to rise. She was sexually aroused and pointed to her generous cleavage which revealed a good portion of her breasts. She said, "Do you want to touch my juicy melons? Go ahead. They're ripe for the picking." Linda was blonde and had white porcelain complexion. She certainly was the type of George. But George had no inkling that he was going to be faced with such a dilemma. They were in a church and all things that happened here were of a religious nature. He was reluctant to give in to Linda's desires due to the stupefied look of the people in the cubicle. George was here for a purpose. He wanted to refresh his memory of the religious upbringing he had when he was a child. Over the course of his adulthood, he felt like he was distancing himself from his childhood tradition. He wanted to relive his happy infancy in the company of his mother and aunts. But they were long gone now because old age had taken a toll on them. This was hardly the venue for an intimate encounter.

Didn't it occur to them that they were being closely watched by church elders? Margaret, the organizer of the prayer meeting, butted in and had this to say, "May I remind the both of you that this erotic behaviour of yours has no place on church grounds. This is not a time for debauchery and deprabed tastes. It would be more appropriate to go to a nightclub or beer garden where you can expose yourself to shameless ruffians." But even though Margaret admonished them in strong terms, George continued to fondle the breasts of Linda and massaged her nipples.

Everyone was taken aback by their provocative behaviour. Pretty soon the two big halves of Linda were in full view of those present. George remarked it was none of his fault because he didn't initiate the sexual overtones. George caressed her breasts touching the erogenous zones which excited her more. He squeezed a nipple and it squirted milk. What to do with this couple who showed no inhibitions displaying moments of intimacy? Margaret spoke with Sister Claire on what measures top take to halt this lascivious demonstration of fleshly desire. They both agreed that one of the two should be ejected from the room to conserve the holy atmosphere of the place. They informed Linda who incited George to touch her, that she was being evicted from the room. George could follow her if he'd like but under no circumstances can they allow lurid scenes like these to play out on church presmises. Linda put her vest on, grabbed her bag and left the room. Everyone was so relieved with the departure of the sex fiend. The place was beginning to look like a circus with her around.

Sister Claire took to the floor and said, «Sorry for that moment of indecency. We never expected it to happen. Let us prepare ourselves for the arrival of the priest by reciting a short prayer which is found on the first page of your prayer books.»

The whole congregation recited a short prayer in unison from the daily missal. Once in a while, they were faced with a recalcitrant member of the congregation who refused to cooperate with the dictates of the church. One time a man came to church with tattered clothes and smelled so bad. The other visitors were having trouble clearing their noses and concentrating. They were giving him the cold shoulder and refused to shake hands with him, He took the hint that he was an obstacle to the objectives of the group and promptly left. No one spoke to him. He must've suffered from mental illness because he was muttering to himself unintelligible things. It is said that worshippers should come to church in their best attire feeling refreshed and smelling good. You should observe the rules on good grooming and etiquette whether in a church, monastery or any other religious institution.

Next up was Stanley Brougham. He was an architect who created the Westmount Plaza, an imposing structure with two glass towers of sixteen storeys high and a mall with restaurants and boutiques in between. It rose gracefully in the skyline of the city with many observers touting it as an architectural gem. He had other designs planned for the city and collaborated with planners and the mayor to map out a blueprint for his future projects. Construction was all set to start on the fall for his luxury condominium project that would use heavy concrete material to withstand natural disasters like earthquakes, cyclones and floods. Mild tremors have been known to occur at this part of the world and seismologists warned inhabitants to prepare for a huge seismic shock that could rattle the city to its foundations. Unleash a tsunami that could wash away everything in its path. His buildings wouldn't vibrate much because he incorporated durable fibreglass at the base to absorb the quake. He also built a big mansion for a rich businessman on solid ground. The facade was made of two massive slabs of stone with iron grilled windows at the center to attract generous amounts of sunlight. It's gate was made of wrought iron electronically controlled and the walls were high and hard to climb. The interior of the house was compartmentalized into many rooms. The master's bedroom was the biggest room.

The dining room and kitchen were spacious and airy with a huge seating capacity. It had an observation deck at the roof of the house, as well as, a helipad where a private chopper would land. It had a large garden that was planted with pine trees and vine trellises underneath the windows. A long driveway led to the entrance of the house where tall fir trees grew and provided a stunning view of the estate. He himself created an amusement park with many rides and a waterfall that fed to a fast-moving river where ticket holders can ride the rapids. It was open only during the spring and summer and closed for maintenance and repairs during the rest of the year. He sought to declare an antebellum residence on Watson Avenue as a heritage site which was built in the eighteenth century. Developers wanted to demolish it to make way for the construction of a new office building. But he opposed their plan asking the city council to halt engineering crews from tearing down the stately manor. A lot of property owners and commercial developers sought his opinion on what to do with old decrepit buildings and houses. He cautioned them not to destroy these vintage pieces of architecture but rather reinforce them with sturdy building materials so they can last another hundred years. These old sytle colonial houses are a testament to a bygone era when settlers were just beginning to fashion the landscape with their crude implements and construction materials. He was collecting photographs of old fashioned houses and buildings later compiled and published as a coffee table book by Doubleday publishing house. He was in charge of refurbishing the downtown core, building overpasses and studying the feasiblity of extending the subway line in many directions. Transit users needed a faster way to get around the city and it was only through the prolongation of subway stops that people would be able to travel. People wanted to avoid traffic jams and the daily chaos that characterized most of the city. The efficiency of a public transit system was a priority of the municipal government and they chose Stanley Brougham as chairman of the planning and executive committee. He would wear a hard hat and work boots when visiting a construction site to shield himself from falling debris and to protect himself from any mishap that could happen. Since they were drilling a hole deep into the bowels of the earth for an extension of the metro line, he took into consideration the recommendations of competent engineers as to the choice of construction materials and equipment. Soon there will be a subway station in all of the boroughs. As more and more commuters will be using the subway line, the traffic in the city will be decongested. He was well remunerated for his work and lived in an elegant home located in a posh suburb.

So what brings these prominent personalities together in a prayer meeting of the Legion of Mary? They wanted to declare their steadfast faith in the Risen Lord and reaffirm their promises to be a loyal servant of the church. When one is pressed for time, it is not unusual to encounter people with other concerns or priorities. Religious matters take a backseat as it is not deemed important enough to merit attention. But these people here attending the meeting want to reinstate the beliefs that they were brought up with and enact the principles of selflessness by giving their time and effort to make the country a better place. A lot of people, not just in the meeting, have volunteered to give generous donations to the church because it is through deeds that one gets to know the spirit of the person, We cannot just mope in one corner and sit in a listless state. We have to get out of our shell and utilize our resources for the benefit of the less fortunate. Margaret sent out letters to wealthy financiers asking them to cooperate in the economic assistance of the needy and destitute. She also sent invitations for them to come to the meeting. This is the reason why a whole lot of them came to answer the call for the reparation of the ills of society. Stanley Brougham, for instance, has designated an old decrepit building that used to be a hospital as a shelter for the homeless.

He brought up the subject during a meeting with city councillors and got the go signal to renovate the place and transofrm it into a refuge for indigents. Especially for homeless people, it is not right to expose them to subzero trempreatures in the frigid weather where they can die of hypothermia. Judith Kramer, the restauranter, promised to provide hot meals to the needy so they didn't have to beg for alms. The emaciated bodies of beggars are the result of the spiralling cost of food which has further endangered their well-being. Someone must be held accountable for the inustice being done to the poor. Through the concerted effort of generous donors, we can ease the plight of our starving fellowmen. That is why the congregation at Sunday mass is urged to give as much money as possible during the offertory. The church, in cooperation with the various hospitals in the city, will conduct free medical assistance to those people not covered by health insurance. They will be providing free medical check ups with follow ups at the hospital, as well as, free dental care. The health of the citizenry is of utmost importance to the church as it strives to lower the mortality rate among the poor. Medical personnel from the Doctors without Borders will be on hand to detect any abnormality, prescribe medication and execute surgical intervention if necessary.

Constable Peter Trent sponsored a gun safety forum to keep guns away from the hands of violent thugs. The ones most vulnerable to gun violence are those people living in the street because they are caught in the crossfire between rival gang members who deal drugs in the street. Domestic violence was also tackled in the forum supplying a hotline number for wives in distress and jeopardy. The church has always maintained a tough stance on criminal elements calling on a crackdown to the proliferation of gun ownership and illegal sales of submachine guns which kill many people in a year. We have to put in place the proper perspectives as dictated by the church which is equal opportunity for all. Revamp the hiring practices of big corporations and medium-sized businesses so there will be less discrimination based on race, gender and religious affiliation. We have to help with the needs of ethnic and religious minorities so they can integrate into society. We cannot just leave them in the outer fringes but rather incorporate them into the mainstream so they can be productive members. There should be no distinction as to the racial background of people because cultural diversity is one of the strong points of the country. We must fight white supremacists whose principles of intolerance and hatred run counter to the church's goals and divide the country.

Stanley Brougham settled snugly in his chair and took out his handkerchief to clean his glasses. Judith Kramer and Frederic Villeneuve sat at the opposite ends waiting to engage him in a conversation. Judith Kramer had a proposition to make and she began with these words, "My restaurant business has plans to expand its operations. We're looking for a place that is accessible to pedestrians and is frequented by a great number of shoppers. The Westmount Plaza which you built is an ideal location for our business since it is situated in a busy downtown area. I was wondering if you have any space available for our restaurant that is looking to open a branch in your area?"

Stanley Brougham replied, «There is a lot of vacant space in the mall, You can contact my agent so you can further negotiate the terms and iron out the details of setting up shop in the building. There's an automatic sprinkler system in case of a fire in the kitchen. Many accidents have happened in cooking areas due to careless handling of equipment and poor storage of goods especially flammable liquids. But I only hope that garbage from your restaurant will not be strewn all over the place. Garbage bins should be neatly placed at the back of the building where garbage trucks pass by to collect them. Dispose properly food residue and compost material in vats so they can be picked up by trucks to be later brought to landfills.

I strongly urge the city council to incinerate all the garbage from stores and restaurants so we can avoid the spread of communicable diseases. We must take steps to exterminate the rat population be keeping the place clean and spotless. Proper sanitation is the key to a healthy environment and we encourage everyone to get rid of garbage correctly. One restaurant was closed due to unhygienic practices. Vermin was seen scuttling in the shelves and flies were seen coming down on the food in the counter. The refrigerator was defective and didn't keep the food fresh. All these things you have to bear in mind so you don't get penalized by the food inspectors. We must prevent the spread of the e. coli bacteria so people don't get sick. Symptoms include vomiting spells, diarrhea and stomach aches. If your customers are stricken by this kind of malady, we have no choice but to padlock your business."

Judith answered, «We follow strict guidelines imposed on us by the food and drug administration. Technicians are on standby alert to upgrade our equipment so we can deliver the best service to our customers. We have very high standards and our restaurant has consistently scored high marks from food inspectors. Our restaurant has earned a five star rating from renowned connoisseurs.»

It was Frederic Villeneuve's turn to talk. "I am from a telemarketing firm called Infotel. We are looking for an office space where we can install phone booths for use by our hired personnel. I wonder if you have any space available in your office building? We are not satisfied with our present location because there is limited parking area for cars."

Stanley Brougham answered, «I have a high rise office building in the city. There are some retail spaces that are vacant. Just be sure that the products you sell are safe and legitimate. I personally don›t like solicitation calls because they call during the oddest hours of the day. Sometimes when we›re eating dinner at home, I get a call selling me tickets to a vacation spot. It is unnerving sometimes that I start to yell on the phone. My number is listed in the directory and that is an invitation for agents to call. But I've already been listed on the Do Not Call list so I expect your supervisor to eliminate my number from your calling list. Some telemarketing firms are a front for fraudulent transactions targeting senior citizens of their lifetime savings. I hope you are a federally approved telemarketing company with no ties to the underworld. You have to be wary about the calls you take because they could be a scam operating in such faraway places like India or Nigeria. Scammers are rarely brought to justice because the money you send them is deposited to a fictitious company. It is almost impossible to trace them In any case, you can contact my agent for further discussion into the subject matter."

Frederic Villeneuve responded to the unfair allegations of Stanley Brougham. "We are a bona fide telemarketing company operating in North America. We are listed in the Securities and Exchange

Commission. The prodcuts we sell are safe and legal and are designed to help businesses thrive and become prosperous. We have a proven track record whereby some businesses we cater to had seen their sales rise in gigantic proportions. We have always stood by the quality of our products and we have never duped anyone into buying run-of-the-mill equipments."

By this time Fatima Hassan had already approached Stanley Brougham and started to speak to him, «There is a scarcity of mosques in the city and there is not a sufficient number to serve the growing Muslim population. I was wondering whether you can build a new mosque that is big and spacious so the Muslims in the city will have another place of worship?"

Stanley Brougham replied, «You have to respect zoning laws and can›t build a place of worship on commercial property. We›ll scout for available terrain maybe in the outskirts so the mosque can be a meeting place for the city›s Muslim population. Recently, mosques have been the target of white supremacists who want to rid the country of Muslim immigrants. They›ve succeeded in instilling fear among the members of the Muslim population.

It is open season and we have to be careful not to provoke the wrath of racists and neo-nazi elements by making an ostentatious display of our faith. I have read the petition of the Muslim council to add a spanking new complex for the faithful. We have to go to the drawing board and plan to build a mosque with a huge dome at the center that will embellish the landscape of the city with its minarets and towers. This country has a multicultural outlook and we have to guarantee every ethnic group the right to freedom of expression."

Fatima crossed her legs and folded her arms. She was glad that she elicited a favorable reaction from the famed architect and hoped that plans would push through for the construction of a new mosque that will showcase Muslim ingenuity.

Next one to approach the architect Stanley Brougham was Galina Ivanovych who didn't mince words on the need for a cultural venue to present the performing arts in a timely fashion. The city sorely lacked a new auditorium for its new season of opera productions and singers were vying for space backstage as the old cultural center didn't provide adequate room for reherasals and performamces.

The dire situation drew a response from the architect. «I have been thinking about this for a long time now. The present auditorium does not have the facilities necessary to bring forth a good performance.

The seating capacity is limited and is positioned obliquely so that some sections of the auditorium don't get a sufficient view of the stage. The acoustics are poor and the sound bounces from the wall creating an echo which can be distracting. The stage isn't level but slouches to one corner affecting the balance of the performers. The orhcestra pit is small and can't accomodate a seventy-two piece orchestra. We have to draw the outline for a new auditorium one that will be an ideal venue for opera performances. I have already spoken to sound engineers and lighting personnel to assure that the new auditorium will have a digital control room to gauge the many shifts of sound and light. There will be a movable stage to facilitate the change of scenery. There will be a bigger seating capacity in the new auditorium, as well as, a large foyer with a high ceiling and a chandelier with swarakovski crystals. There will be bigger seats so you'll have ample room to stretch your legs unlike in the old auditorium where you can hardly move. We have to plan the design carefully and methodically because we don't want to be criticized of shoddy workmanship. It will be a multi-level opera house with balconies to the side, the orchestra at ground level and the mezzanine at the middle. You won't need to bring binoculars because everyone will have a perfect view from their seat."

The priest entered the cubicle and the people hurriedly went to their proper places. They took their respective seats and stopped moving about. There was so much conversation going on and a flurry of activities that it resembled more like a social club than a prayer meeting. People were milling around the architect because there were things they wanted to discuss with him. Now that the priest was present, there was a hush that descended on the congregation and everyone fell silent. Margaret called to order the minutes of the meeting. She submitted a report to the priest and spoke about the objectives of the group. The attendance was checked and there were many visitors this time. She enjoined everyone to prepare themselves for prayer and to meditate on the glorious mysteries of the rosary. Everyone was still and took out the guide on how to say the rosary. Margaret lit the two candles that were situated on the opposite ends of the statue of the Virgin Mary. When everything became clear that everyone was ready to pray, the priest took out his rosary and started reciting the prayer. The priest's name was Fr. John Rifkin who had long years of service with the church. He started out as a novice in a monastery where he learned to obey his superiors and to get closer to God through the recitation of prayers. He was well-suited to the austere lifestyle of the monastery having only the basic necessities and never needing luxury items such as a fancy bed or porcelain plates and silverware, He slept in a simple cot in a room which he shared with two other monks. He was in his early sixties with a receding hairline that was a sign that age was creeping up on him. Everyone in the room recited the Hail Mary from memory except Fatima Hassan who was not familiar with the rosary. Margaret gave her a pamphlet on the rosary so she can join in the recitation of the prayers. She just stared at it, dawdled and said nothing. She wasn't converted yet to the Catholic faith but sat as a visitor observing the rituals practiced by believers. It is hard to convert Muslim people into the Catholic religion because they have many misconceptions regarding the veracity of the faith as the one true religion. In the first place, she was deeply involved in her religion, wearing a hijab and exhorting all Muslims to turn towards Mecca to pray. She made a pilgrimage to the Muslim holy site where she reiterated her vows to be a devout Muslim woman. Margaret warned Fatima that if she refused to participate in the prayers, she might just as well leave. They have no place for obdurate sit-ins with their condescending attitude towards the Catholic faith. Fatima took her coat, rose from her seat and left the chair vacant.

After saying the rosary, Fr. Rifkin led the group in the benediction of the church and its servants through the intercession of the angels and saints. They also prayed for the canonization of Fr. Casimir Welland, a nineteenth century Franciscan priest who oversaw the construction of the church and became a staunch defender of the goals of the church which was to bind into one the differeing viewpoints of the members of the clergy so they can function into one cohesive unit. After the prayer ended, Fr. Rifkin asked several of those present to recount the way in which they rediscovered their faith in the Risen Lord. It was important to renew the promises they made at baptism and to be imbued with the spirit of God so they can act according to His will. Several of them answered that they felt a void in their lives that could only be filled by the presence of a divine power. The architect, for instance, said that the skyscrapers he built touched the heavens and it only goes to show that we are just a breath away from reaching the dwelling place of God. The opera singer, Galina Ivanovych, stated that she'd sing the soprano roles in religious oratorios to give glory to God. Janet Serrano, the president's daughter, promised that she won't have any more affairs with married men but try to settle down with a decent single man. The rest of the interlocutors made different promises to the priest and Margaret took note of them in her minutes of the meeting.

Fr. John Rifkin worked closely with the law enforcement agency to maintain peace and order in the community. He would exhange information with police officers to keep abreast with events that were happening so he could gauge the needs of the community. He was also concerned about the security in the streets urging police officers to patrol the area. Whenever he'd see idle youths loitering in the streets, he'd call their attention and order them to disperse and go home. For all we know they might be dealing with drugs and luring young girls to work as prostitutes, He›d take down their names and their social insurance numbers to be registered as juvenile delinquents or unemployed youths up for review to see if they have any criminal antecedents. He was concerned about many things regarding the upkeep of the church. He asked Margaret who kept the purse strings of the parish whether she had already hired a gardener to prune the branches and leaves of the trees and bushes and to cut down the grass. Weeds and tall grasses have grown in places where they shouldn't be like in flower beds or along the periphery of the church. These unwanted herbs should be uprooted or mowed down. Also, the facade of the church needs a little refurbishing. The paint on the walls were cracking dry due to the fluctuations of the temperature in the earth's atmosphere.

It needed a new coat of paint to make the church more attractive and more pleasant to see. Food booths will be installed at the front lawn of the church to mark the country's independence day celebrations. Big garbage bins should be placed at all corners of the church so people don't litter the church grounds with food wrappers, styrofoam cups and paper plates. Margaret ordered fresh flowers from a well-known florist to decorate the altar for its forthcoming Easter celebration. The pews needed a fresh layer of varnish so that they will be all spruced up in time for Sunday mass. The bathrooms were all cleaned and washed with detergent and disinfectant by janitors who also placed menthol stubs in urinals to get rid of the stench. There were notices on the walls to encourage users of the bathroom to clean up after use. But the theme that most preoccupied Fr. John Rifkin was the security on the premises of the church. Guards would be stationed at the entrance of the church inspecting bags and knapsacks that could contain hidden explosives. Recently, there has been a spate of bomb attacks on churches in Sri Lanka and the authorities are wary about bad elements who want to inflict damage and casualty on churchgoers. Although the probability of a bomb attack on churches in North America is low due to the rigorous process of double checking the identity and background of Muslim immigrants. Muslim extremists are believed to be the ones behind the bomb attacks in Sri Lanka. You have to abide by the law and put everything in the proper perspective. Don't go about breaking the law because the consequences of your ill-conceived actions are harsh and can entail a prison sentence. One time a wanted criminal went into the confessional and confessed of his involvement in a crime. The priest calmly told him to give himself up to the authorities. Fr. John Rifkin teamed up with computer analysts to create a website for the church. In this era of social media, you have to be up-to-date on the methods of communication. It would be a site where they could entertain queries from people surfing on the web. They could widen their network by answering questions from curious onlookers who wanted to dig deeper into the teachings of the Catholic church. The address and phone number would be listed on the website so that visitors would know how to reach them. He had just finished writing a book about the history of the church and its relevance to the needs of the community in the twenty-first century. He was discussing the final details with the editors of a publishing firm to include photographs he unearthed in the archives that featured the team behind the construction of the church, as well as, pictures of the church taken at different angles.

Meanwhile, in another part of town right after sundown, Roger Sison, the prime suspect in the slaying of William Gomez, his erstwhile lover, went inside a bar and sat on a stool. Sweat was trickling across his forehead and he kneaded his temples to soothe his tired mind. He ordered a jigger of brandy on the rocks from a female bartender who also attended to the order of other clients. There were a few tables at the bar occupied by happy-go-lucky customers who were drinking beer, slurping the froth with their tongues, laughing and joking with their friends. Roger wasn't a habitual drinker, just a glass of alcohol to diffuse the tension in his body. In comes a thirty-two year old strawberry blonde girl who sits beside him. She was wearing short pants and a t-shirt with spaghetti straps to beat the heat of the summer. She initiated the conversation. "You look uptight and highly strung. Relax a bit and enjoy the highly-charged particles of air that seep through the windows. This isn't the rain forest in the Amazon but a bustling metropolis with many shops and bistros to go to. Do you have some weed by any chance? I'd like to smoke a joint before I get back on the road."

Roger replied, «Sorry, I don›t do drugs. I›m a firm believer in clean living, having a balanced diet and enjoy a drink or two every once in a while.»

The girl corrected Roger, «Marijuana has been legal since October. A lot of people have been getting high on weed. A different kind of lifestyle because we need to calibrate our set of priorities. I don›t do hard stuff though like meth or crack cocaine unless you want to end up in a dumpster. People are busy trying to earn a buck. They have no time for idle chatter or flirt at a bar. But that doesn›t mean we can›t enjoy ourselves by letting our guard down and order a few drinks.»

The bartender approached the girl and told her the drinks were on the house. Her winsome company enlivened the room and the establishment wanted to show appreciation for her cheerful presence. She ordered a beer in a mug that flowed from a switch in the counter. There were many bottles of liquor all lined up at the bar set against a mirror that stretched from wall to wall.

The girl started to speak again. «I don›t mind when people call me a slut. I ran away from home at a young age due to an abusive father who threw fits of violence because he was under the influence. I had to fend for myself while I lived in the streets. I learned the hard way and fell into bad company. I worked for a pimp, selling my body for a pittance of what I was worth. I›m more mature now but still working in the streets. Maybe we could check into a motel or somewhere and have an intimate encounter?»

A hand job will cost you fifty dollars while full intercourse will set you back two hundred bucks." She had blue eyeliner on and red smudges on her cheeks. She looked like a rag doll, one that little girls drag along to garden parties to play tea time with.

Roger revealed a bit of himself. «I›m a stripper myself offering sexual gratification in exchange for money. I›m a bit hard up on cash and can›t pay fot the favors you ask. Maybe you can come see me sometimes. I work at the Adonis club for a mixed bag of clients. So if you know anyone who needs to get his rocks off, just come see me. We're both in the same boat. I perform on the dance floor and move to the rhythm of the music. Aside from a flat rate salary, I get tips from customers. I scratch the surface, working my butt off and scrape together wads of twenty dollar bills to sustain my substandard level of living. Wish I can find a benefactor who'll help me out."

Just then a man in a suit and tie approached the girl and offered to buy her a drink if she would share his table and keep him company. She relented and left Roger alone. It was easier to get by if you were a woman because you had a hole between your legs ready to be rammed by a hard tool. The wet labia would be a natural lubricant for a man pumping his dick in and out the crevice with pure orgasm. Even during the Japanese invasion, soldiers needed comfort women to satisfy their craving for human flesh.

Roger ordered another drink. This time a tall glass of beer because he was feeling disturbed. Images of William splayed on the bed with a big gash on his throat kept recurring in his mind. His despicable deed was gnawing in his conscience and tried to brush it off with a mouthful of alcohol. The bartender gave him a small plate of olives and sardines and said that the girl he was talking to got tabled. The bar is for mingling with other people to pass away the time. Just then a mulatto man, the same color of skin, sat beside Roger and introduced himself. "My name Philip Whitmore. A tourist from the Caribbean savoring the varied delights of the city. The luxury ship I was riding just docked yesterday and I have time to rub elbows with the native inhabitants. May I join you?"

Roger answered, «Not at all, Take a seat. It›s not everyday I come across a sightseer who needs a guide to show him around. Coming to a bar is a good place to start because at least you can socialize with other customers over a couple of drinks."

Philip commented, «You flex your muscles like a pro. I guess you spend many hours at the gym.» He said this with sexual overtones.

Roger replied, «Not exactly. I have to be in fine form because I›m a dancer by profession. I have to impress the audience by my looks and having rugged biceps and fully developed pectoral muscles is one way of grabbing their attention. I hope you have time to see my performance."

Philip ran his fingers along the upper body of Roger, feeling his muscles and grasping the contours of his chest. Philip massaged his shoulders and Roger acquiesced to the amorous overture of Philip. Roger eased his weary joints due to the gentle strokes of Philip›s hands. But there was still the fear of being caught by police that troubled Roger. How long before he gets traced by law enforcement and gets locked up in a jail cell?

Roger confided to his new friend Philip Whitmore. «I›m in a kind of a fix. Ruthless elements are out to catch me and I have to constantly flee for my life. My situation is precarious and don›t know if I›ll live another day. Maybe you could take me with you back home in the Caribbean where I›ll be safe from harm.»

Philip bent over to give Roger a kiss, right smack on the lips «I›ll be leaving in a week. Make sure your papers are in order and I›ll buy you a ticket for the cruise ship. Talk about fatal attraction. The moment I came in that door, I knew you were the one for me.»

JUst then the bartender noticed that something was awry. She searched deep into the recesses of her mind and connected the dots together.

She was convinced that it was Roger's face she saw in the poster for a wanted criminal. The composite sketch revealed striking similarities and there was no mistaking that the man at the bar was the suspect in a murder case. The bartender confronted Roger with her assumption and told him not to move while she called the police. Consumed with anger and rage at being tagged as the culprit in a sensational case, Roger stood up from his stool, took an ice pick from the bucket and stabbed the bartender in her chest. The bartender gasped for air and knocked down several bottles as she struggled with her life. Blood oozed out of her body staining her shirt and apron before finally slumping to the ground. The customers in the room screamed in horror as they took cover from the ensuing scuffle. Philip was speechless at having witnessed a case of physical assault and told Roger that he needed to go abroad with him to excape incriminating evidence to be presented in a court of law. He didn't care if he was coddling a criminal. Point is he was madly in love with Roger. Both of them scampered out of the bar and rode a taxi to an unknown destination. Soon the police came and scoured the place interviewing customers who had seen the bar brawl. Their description of the assailant matched the face in the poster but couldn't come up with a name.

At the Adonis club, rehearsals were underway for tonight's presentation. The dancers all lined up the stage including Roger and a bunch of other men. They were told to do limbering exercises before executing their synchronized number. Roger was doing push ups while the others were alternately doing sit ups and bending exercises. Some were practicing their reverse flip. The only props they had were chairs. The director called their attention and signalled that the rehearsal would start. They danced to the song Footloose by Kenny Loggins as it blared from the speakers. Each dancer would have their turn at the center stage ripping the buttons of the pants located at the side. They were especially fabricated for strip tease acts to show some skin to the audience. None of them wore shirts but bared their chests for the duration of the performance. At the beat of the music, everyone jumped and did a somersault in the air. Later, they did cartwheels and hand stands. One performer did breakdancing when it was his turn at the center. When they ripped their pants off, they were wearing nothing but a g-string. Their buttocks were naked as they had their backs to the stage. Later during the show, the dancers would go from table to table so customers could wiggle in paper money inside their underwear.

Philip was at the back sitting on a chair drinking a margarita. He laid down his glass on the table and applauded heartily. He blew kisses at the dancers and waved his hand at Roger. The director called for a halt to the rehearsal and said the number was well executed. He told the dancers to rest for tonight's performance. Roger approached Philip and sat at his side. Philip said he was mesmerized by the dance routine and couldn't have been more pleased with Roger's participation. They were sure to get curtain calls and requests for an encore presentation. If only they'd put on cowboy hats to make it look more western. On this same street, there was a nightclub that featured drag queens. Philip suggested that they check it out to see men fully made up as women wearing gaudy dresses with beads and feathers. They had fancy wigs on in shades of red, pink and yellow. They had garish make up on with false eyelashes, red blush on their cheeks and thick lipstick that overstepped the outline of the lips. All to make his stay in the country more memorable and exciting.

There was a room at the back of the club where dancers would bring their clients for some erotic interlude. The room was vacant and Roger and Philip lied down on the bed face to face Philip brushed aside the hair of Roger to get a clearer view of his eyes. He said, "I don't know what drew me to come to these foreign shores. A sense of adventure or a longing to explore other lands. I am sure glad I found you because it was worth the trip. To have and to hold you. I don't ever want to let you go. You're gonna like the Caribbean. Bathe in the waterfalls, get a bronzed tan from the radiant sun and peel a banana from a tree that grows in the wild. The pace of life is slow. You ride a horse drawn buggy around the town, sip coconut juice from a husk and frolic in the white sandy beaches. You can even go scuba diving in the clear blue waters of the ocean as you marvel on the pink and blue corals that line the reef. Just be careful of the sharks that swim in the water. Always have a dinghy not far from you so you can escape its hungry jaws. As for the bartender you killed, the long arm of law can't reach you there. You'll be under an assumed identity. I have the passport of a friend of mine who never made it to the ship. You can tamper with the passport and insert your photo. You'll go through customs in a wink of an eye. When you get to the Carribean, you won't have to work because everything will be at your disposal. Just live in a hut by the beach and watch the waves roll by. You'll have warm weather all year round so you won't shiver in the cold. Live as the natives do. You'll find them warm and affectionate and ready to lend a helping hand. Be ready in a week. I'll come pick you up."

Roger nodded in assent and was grateful for having given the chance to redo his life. He never thought he›d meet a good Samaritan who›d lift him from the squalor he was living in. A new horizon lay in front of him. He better not miss the boat, no pun intended, that would bring him to a more hospitable land.

The morning after the performance, Roger went to the photographer›s studio to have his passport photo taken. He received a cordial reception from a middle-aged man who fulfilled his request. He was carrying the passport that Philip handed him to be tamperred with his photo in place of the rightful holder. He could hardly figure out how to tell the photographer of his request if he was capable of falsifying it and done neatly. The photographer wasn't surprised at all because he had altered passports several times before. He assured Roger that he could do a good job and asked a fee of fifty dollars up front. Roger paid him and he went to work in a jiffy. The process was painstaking as he gathered all the vials containing liquids that were necessary in the preparation. First he uncorked a fast-acting paint thinner to dissolve the adhesive on the page indicated.

Next he applied a dab of acetone to lift the old picture from the page. So far so good as he dried the page with a hair blower to get rid of the moisture. The page was now ready for the insertion of Roger's photo. The process took no more than twenty minutes. He reapplied adhesive with the new picture and sealed the page with the plastic covering. At last Roger had a passport with his photo on it. The photographer swore that he'd keep the matter confidential and that he wouldn't leak the information about the faked passport to the authorities. It is stated at the back of the passport that said document was the property of the state and that any misrepresentation was an infraction of the law. Roger walked out of the studio a happy man, confident that he could board the vessel with the least hassle. A tampered passport was the only way Roger could lay his hands on a travel document. He didn't have the required documents needed to apply for a new passport. He lacked identification cards and did not possess a birth certificate. The circumstances of his birth were enveloped in mystery as he was delivered into this world by a midwife who didn't register him with any hospital. To top it all, Roger was carrying a foreign passport so he'd never get flagged down by a customs officer.

Customs and immigration were strict with their own citizens. Aside from passports, the bearer must present a valid visa of the country they were headed to. Impertinent questions were asked at the desk like showing proof of funds for the trip and the address of the place he was going to stay in. The question and answer portion was nerve-wracking especially for one who was not briefed on how to respond beforehand. The luggages of the passengers were strip-searched for the presence of aerosol spray cans or bottles containing corrosive substances. The stale air and the unregulated temperature of the baggage compartment can adversely react with flammable liquids. Only crew members were allowed into the captain's deck. No one was to interfere with the steering wheel of the captain as he guided the ship towards the vast expanse of the ocean. Some crew members were armed with pistols and submachine guns to protect themselves from pirates who would hop aboard unannounced. This has happened several times with oil tankers which were hijacked by Somali pirates in exchange for a hefty ransom. In the unlikely event of a hijack, the captain would contact control tower to dispatch aircraft carriers to battle it out with the pirates.

It was the first trip abroad for Roger so he was very excited about the voyage. All his life he knew nothing but filth and grime. He'd do odd jobs like cleaning toilets and mopping floors until he met an agent who persuaded him to be a dancer. He got his break doing lewd dances at a sleazy joint until he was given a job at the club. Still as a dancer but in a more decent venue. He had no choice but to flee this time because he was a fugitive from justice. He would wake up at night screaming because of a bad dream. But it was reality kicking in and he had to think of a way to surmount it. He was headed for the hotel where Philip stayed. There to spend the rest of the day until their departure to a land where he would no longer have to live in the shadows. The sun never shone so brightly as it did now as there was a promise of a better tomorrow. He tried to clear his head from morbid thoughts. His past seemed to haunt him but soon he'd find himself in a totally different surrounding. He had no regrets about what he did to William. He had it coming to him. He was a flirt and a cheat. Nothing between heaven and earth can stop him from achieving his goal of leaving the miserable life behind. No one could put him behind bars to face a trial that was more like a farce and a test of wills. He who laughs las, laughs best. The criminal justice system had much to be desired. He didn't want to be treated like an animal paraded before the press. He deserved a life of dignity and honor.

Roger knocked on the door of the hotel suite. Philip opened the door and ushered him into the room. He hugged Roger tightly and whispered sweet words to his ear. Tomorrow was the day of reckoning when like other foreign nationals, Roger would just slip by the cordon where customs officers and security personnel will scrutinize the papers of the travellers. The island in the Caribbean where they were headed was home to some species of birds that didn't have a natural defense mechanism against predatory creatures like snakes and domesticated cats. They were flightless birds like dodos or New Zealand wren that were essentially ground dwellers and were in danger of extinction if no measures were taken to protect it. They had short wingspan and were clumsy fliers.

Roger only had one suitcase and a carry-on bag which contained some clothing and toiletries. Roger showed the passport to Philip and he remarked that it was expertly done. Enough to fool even the most trained eye. There were no rough edges and the plastic was skillfully glued to the page. From now on Roger would be known as Tony Wingfield, aged 34 and domiciled in the Caribbean. It was the name inscribed in the passport and the name he would respond to in case the officer would ask him questions. Everything that Roger owned was in that small suitcase.

He was a penniless man who was starting from scratch. Philip handed him his ticket and boarding pass which Roger accepted with cries of joy. "How can I ever repay you?" went Roger. Philip replied, "Just don't waste this opportunity for a fresh start. Don't go around breaking old men's hearts." Philip explained to Roger that the attitude towards gay men was becoming more and more tolerant. It was not uncommon to see two men hold hands promenading in the street. There were nightclubs in the town that were frequented by gay men. Bars would serve cocktails until daybreak. He'd find himself quite at home in the island. There where the rubber trees grow and the humming of the crickets start at dusk. It was time to go to sleep now because they had to get up early in the morning to board the luxury cruise liner. Everything was paid for and the only thing that worried Roger was the standing order for his arrest. He left a trail of debris and the close circuit TV at the bar probably took a good snapshot of him. But he was confident he could pull this one through because the video of him at the bar was grainy and of poor quality. There were many people at the pub and the confusion that took place after the incident left the customers scurrying for safety. it could have been anyone because there were many people in close proximity to the bartender.

But this was the big day when Roger and Philip headed to the pier where the ship was docked. When they got to the pier, they had to wait in line like the rest of the passengers to have their tickets validated, boarding passes inspected and passports reviewed. The engine of the ship was running as it blew steam up into the air. The line moved slowly as the luggages went through a conveyor belt that would bring it to an x-ray machine. Even after that the personal effects of the passengers were carefully inspected. Philip had slid through the customs desk like a wraith and answered only a few questions like "How did you like your stay?" or "would you recommend this trip to your family and friends back home?"

Rate your answer between one and five, five being the most likely. It was like answering a survey which as a matter of fact it was. It was Roger's turn at the desk of the officer. The officer told him to take off his sunglasses to get a better view of the face. Noticing that according to his passport, he was a foreign national, the officer asked him the same questions. After getting a few quick answers, the officer waived further questioning and cleared him through the entrance of the ship. As the vessel lifted its anchor, it began to sail away and Roger waved at the reception committee below. He began his long jouney away from the slums he'd grown to despise.

Linda Duvalier, the foxy woman who was expelled from the Legion of Mary prayer meeting, was back in the limelight as a guest at a dating game show. The show was hosted by Bob Mackey, a popular TV presenter who anchored several other TV programs. There were three male contestants who were vying for the love and affection of Linda and based on their answers, Linda would get to choose only one. There was a wall that separated Linda from the three contestants so she didn't know how they look like. She'd have to cull from the group, use her intuition and pick the one that stands out the most. The show was taped from a live audience who could help Linda choose the most likely candidate.

Linda: «What do you expect on a first date? What will you do to impress me?»

Contestant no. 1: «I›ll wine and dine you. Take you to a fancy restaurant where we can get to know one another through candle light and glasses of wine. We can sit in front of a fireplace and wrap ourselves in blankets to keep warm. We›ll cuddle up together and I›ll regale you with stories of my adventures. By day we can go cycling together at Stanley park, feed the pigeons with bread crumbs while sitting on a bench enjoying the sunshine of springtime weather. I›d shower you with kisses if you›ll let me. Later, when we get to know each other a little more, we can go romping in a beach collecting seashells and rowing a canoe to the pale blue yonder."

Linda: «That›s a lot of things to do. Are you sure you won›t tire of me? I will spend a lot of your precious time.»

Contestant no. 1: «It›s all worth it for a pretty girl like you. I presume you have a lovely face otherwise you wouldn›t be the object of this contest. I always have time to spare to be with attractive women. I don›t mind having an affair with a single woman. As long as you›re not attached with anyone, we can go out as many times as you want.»

The same question for the next contestant.

Contestant no. 2: «I›ll wrap you around my arms and give you a hearty kiss. I›ll take you to my flat to show you the various trophies I won during weightlifting competitions. If you›re light enough, I can lift you with a single arm just to show you my physical strength. Later, we can go to a bar, order tequila and join the others at their table to erupt into a raucous laughter. We›ll have a swell time sharing stories of our human existence. I›ll introduce you to my buddies so you can figure out how well-connected I am. I like my friends to go around in circles rubbing elbows with one another.»

Linda: «That›s a fun way to start a date. How do you know I›ll be accepted by your group of friends?»

Contestant no. 2: "I know you'll fit the description of a beautiful woman. Preferably blonde hair and blue eyes. I hate it when women cut their hair short. It just doesn't suit them. I can see it clearly now. You'll be a knockout to my cirlce of friends."

The same question for the last contestant.

Contestant no. 3: ‹I›ll take you for a ride in my porsche. We can go to a drive-in movie and snuggle up in the dark. You'll let me caress your soft skin. No time to waste for a man in a hurry like me. We'll get down to business and you'll lower your top for me to ogle at your creamy delights. You're the cherry on top of a cake, the ribbon that ties the loose ends."

Linda: «How very presumptuous of you, You act very fast for a first date. What if we're not compatible?"

Contestant no. 3: «By the sound of your voice, you seem to be an affable woman. You have no hang ups about liking men with a fondness for the female form. I won›t drop you like a hot potato. I give you my word that I›ll respect and satisfy your wishes.»

Bob Mackey: «There you have it, the answers of our three male contestants. More questions will come come your way in a little while. The audience will have a chance to vote for the contestant they think is most suited to the female searcher. But first, a word from our sponsors."

The commercials ended and the show resumed its programming. Linda posed her second question.

Linda: «What if we get into a serious relationship and I get pregnant, will you marry me?»

Contestant no. 1: «I›d drop all my baggage on the floor, rush you to the altar and marry you in front of a priest. I won›t leave you to your own devices but make room in my house for you to sleep in. I›ll take responsibility for the action that I took and follow you through the completion of your pregnancy. When the baby does come out of your tummy, we›ll give it a name and a loving home. I›m financially capable of feeding a family and fully prepared to tackle the role of a father.»

Linda: «That›s nice to hear. At least you won›t leave me by the wayside. You›re a man of honor. I›ll take note of it.»

Contestant no. 2: «I›m still too young to be a father. There›s still a lot of girls out there waiting to be explored and I›d like to enjoy my days as a bachelor before I plunge myself into marriage. In the event that you do get pregnant on account of my carelessness, I›ll urge you to interrupt your prenancy so you'll be free to match up with other single men."

Linda: «What you›re looking for is a fling. I don›t want to be tied up with one man but would rather have the option to date other men.»

Contestant no. 3: "I'll give my name to the baby and sign all the necessary documents so I'll be known as the father. But I won't marry you or put a ring on your finger. I'll give you financial support so you can raise the baby and call him your own. But due to other commitments, I won't be able to be at your side and watch the baby grow. Just choose me if you want to have a wonderful time. I should take the necessary precautions so you don't find yourself in an awkward situation."

Linda: «I deplore the fact that you won›t be able to fulfill your obligation as father to the child. Paperwork means nothing if you can›t abide by your duty to look after the child. You want me to be a single mother who›ll work my butt out just so you can be free to do whatever you please.»

Bob Mackey: "Here's the last question from our female searcher. I hope you have by now come up with your choice. Let's see if this last part sways your judgement."

Linda: «What attracts you most about a woman? What part of a woman excites you most?»

Contestant no. 1: «Everything in a woman excites me. From the scent of her perfume to the size of her bra. From the shampoo she uses on her hair to the lotion she uses on her skin. From the designer clothes she wears to the jewelry that adorns her body. I like a statuesque beauty who›ll let me touch her most intimate parts.»

Linda: "You obviously like the physical aspects of a woman."

Contestant no. 2: «I am fascinated by the charms of a woman. The enigmatic smile of a Mona Lisa, the elegant bearing of a Venus de Milo and the indescribable beauty of Aphrodite that is so hard to put into words. The way she laughs and the way she walks down the aisle with her poise and calm demeanor. I›ll choose the fairest of them all to be my bride at the appropriate time.»

Contestant no. 3: «The woman I most look up to is my mother because she was the one who brought me into this world. All women have the gift of bearing children and they should be congratulated on this unrivalled feat. No one can replace the love of a mother and it is with this in mind that I have come to idolize women.»

Bob Mackey: «There you have it, the final answers of our three contestants. Based on their answers, you will be able to figure out which of the three best suits the female searcher. Only one of the three gets to be paired with the woman at the center of it all. The one you choose will spend a week›s vacation with the female searcher at the Club Med hotel and spa. They will get free meals, facials and massage treatments courtesy of Aladdin tours. But before we conclude, I›m going to ask all three contestants a different question each and the contestant who gives the best response wins a five hundred dollar gift certificate from Canadian Tire.»

Bob Mackey: "Now to the last part of the program. I will start in reverse order and ask contestant no. 3 first. Your question is: What is your idea of a beautiful woman? How do you expect the woman of your dreams to look like?"

Contestant no. 3: «Physical appearance isn›t all that important to me. You can pair me off with a black woman with rough features and I›ll still be happy. What matters is the inner beauty or the personality of the individual. Is she kind and considerate? Is she good at housekeeping? Does she leave the water running and never close the faucet? Does she go into a rage when something's not done? Does she look after her man with attention and diligence? I like to come home to a house that is neat and tidy. Have the meals prepared and get tucked into bed after a pleasant conversation. I have an aversion towards body odor so she shouldn't smell rancid. Perhaps apply a pine scented cologne so that when I nuzzle up to her in bed, I can be in the arms of a sweet-smelling woman. She's the lady of the house so she should be attentive to all the details. There's a new challenge as each day passes and I expect her to face it with the correct attitude."

Bob Mackey: «Well said contestant no. 3. Now let›s move on to contestant no. 1. We know that the mother can be the driving force in our lives. We idolize her and pay reverence to her.

But what if she disapproves of the girl you're dating and tells you to stop seeing her? Do you obey your mother or do you defy her orders and go on seeing the girl?"

Contestant no. 1: «Much as I love my mother, I have to go with the prodding of my heart. I have to answer the knock on the door and follow her who is the light of my life. If you let other people run your life, they›ll ruin the dreams you nurtured and shred it into bits and pieces. What›s important is to stand your ground and don›t let anyone blow the candle that you lit. The woman that I woo will illuminate my life and we should not let anyone obscure the glow that the love of your life gives. A woman is a joy to behold and don›t let anyone, not even your mother, get in the way between you and your prized possession. Never take the woman for granted but reassure her that you will respect your commitments and that you›re in it for the long haul.»

Bob Mackey: «And now a question for contestant no. 2: You›ve fallen in love with a woman other than your wife. Do you dump your wife and go with your mistress or do you keep it a secret and keep the two women?»

Contestant no. 2: «I don›t want to be charged with bigamy in a court of law. Either I initiate divorce proceedings due to irreconcilable differences or quit seeing my mistress due to reasons of infidelity. A man was born for one woman only. It's like skipping a chapter of a book, never being able to read it entirely. I know of some men who have mistresses. They're in a difficult situation trying to make both ends meet. I wouldn't want to be in their shoes."

Bob Mackey: «There you have it, the answers of our three male contestants. We will reveal the winner of this contest after the commercial break. Meanwhile, get close to your touch screen computer terminals because voting begins now. It won›t be long until the results appear on your TV screen. Stay tuned for the results.»

Commercials of Tide detergent, Tim Hortons and 6/49 Lottery appear on the TV screen. After the break, it›s back to the show.

Bob Mackey: «I have here the winner of the five hundred dollar gift certificate. It goes to none other than contestant no.3» He shakes the hand of contestant no. 3 and hands him the envelope. "And now for the results of the dating game. Thirteen per cent voted for contestant no. 3, thirty per cent voted for contestant no. 2, and fifty seven per cent voted for contestant no. 1. I will divulge the identity of the winner. He is none other than Julian Labrecque, a financial consultant from the Laurentian bank. Julian meet Linda Duvalier. The others that were not chosen are Bruce Collins, an accountant from the firm Price and Waterhouse and Steven Hadley, a gym instructor."

The two meet and Julian had such a magnetic personality that Linda was attracted to him right away. End of show.

Jonas was back in the non-descript, ramshackle family home. It was quite a big house. A room for each sibling. The smell of garlic was wafting through the air as the cook was busy preparing a plate of gambas which was a concoction of shrimps immersed in tomato sauce. His brother Jack was on the warpath making his life unbearable. While Jonas was resting in his room, Jack mentioned that he would kill him. Jonas was not about to take his threats lightly. He was going to do do something about it so his brother never gets up again. Was he going to ask for Jack's forgiveness or was he going to finish him off? Did he have the courage to put a bullet through his head or would Jack acquiesce and give him another chance? Jonas's brother Manuel said to steer clear of Jack and avoid his presence. But how can you avoid his company if you were all living in the same house? The priest said that most troubles occur among the people in the house. Either you vacate the presmises or seize the opportunity to patch up differences. But the conflict between the two brothers reached a point of no return and there was no way to bury the hatchet. There was only going to be one victor who'd stand tall amid the rubble. Will Jonas run away to save himself from destruction or will he confront Jack for one last time to settle the score? When everyone was away, he tiptoed to Jack's room with the purpose of instigating a showdown.

It happened all too fast like a flame on a candle that inadvertently set the house on fire. He knocked on the door and Jack answered. With much trepidation but with a steel determination, Jonas pointed a gun at him. Before Jack could close the door to deflect the shots, Jonas fired a gun at him and hit his head. The surface of Jack's skull caved in as the bullet penetrated deep into the cranium. Jonas never thought he could do it, pull the trigger on his mortal enemy. The body of Jack fell to the ground lifeless and blood oozed out of the fatal wound to the forehead. His face was covered with blood and his mouth was open as if he panicked to save himself from Jonas's act of revenge.

Police officers would soon descend upon the family home so Jonas had to act quickly to cover up his deed. He took out a handkerchief and wiped his fingerprints from the revolver. He placed the revolver perfectly on Jack›s right hand to make it look like he pulled the trigger on himself. The index finger on the trigger and the thumb around the base. Jonas left the family home momentarily and went to watch a movie.

Cecille discovered the body of Jack because the door was unlocked. The air conditioner was running and there were paint brushes on the easel that Jack was working on. She called the police to investigate the incident. There were no witnesses and it was reported that Jack died of a single gunshot wound to the head.

Foul play was suspected but could not be proven without a reasonable doubt. What could have been the motive for killing Jack? Was it an attempted robbery gone wrong? Or did anyone carry a grudge towards this brute? Jonas washed his hands with soap to get rid of the gun powder. The death of Jack was ruled an apparent suicide because he was found holding the gun. If only Jack confided to Cecille about his problems this never would have happened. If it was a suicide, what could have driven Jack to take his own life? Jonas was off the hook and was never implicated in the death of his brother. Jonas was laughing vociferously to himself, jubilant that no one pointed a finger at him. It was a product of his skillful ingenuity and deft handling of a murder he had been planning for quite some time now. The body was carried out in a stretcher draped in a white cloth from head to toe. What baffled the mind of the police detective was why he didn't leave a suicide note. Suicide victims usually write last minute letters to their loved ones explainging the reason for ending their lives. Jonas lit a bonfire at the back of the house and incinerated the blood-splattered clothes he wore at the time of the murder. Jonas had to get rid of all the evidence that can be used against him. With Jack gone, Jonas danced the night away because he felt as if a thorn had been plucked from the soles of his feet.

Jonas was back in the spotlight again this time as an object of lust by his sister Gilda. Gilda had an unnatural attraction for her borhter which made Jonas uneasy. She would call Jonas from her bedroom window overlooking the patio and expose her breasts. Jonas was flustered and put in a state of agitated confusion. He wanted to throw up due to the overt invitation for a sexual encounter with his blood relative. The attraction had been building up. First, Gilda would praise the looks of Jonas asking that he lend his alluring appearance to her company. Then she would comment on the curls of his sideburns that made her want to touch it. Next she would go around in her nightie breathing heavily making strange noises as if she was in the throes of ecstasy outside Jonas's bedroom door. Jonas had the shock of his lifetime whe he opened the door to deliver the pizza she ordered and saw her taking a nap without her panties. He only wanted a platonic relationship with his sister, a case of brotherly love to further weld the family together. But the opposite was happening. The stimulus was so great that soon Jonas was having fantasies about her. He confided his predicament to his best friend Larry and told him maybe he needed a night out with a male prostitute. Larry influenced Jonas into being a homosexual. He was relatively inexperienced with matters relating to women.

He was more familiar with cuddling up to masculine bodies and felating penises. Everybody knows Jonas was gay but inspite of that Gilda was still pushing for an illicit relationship with her borhter. Larry leaked the dirty little secret to the media and soon TV programs were playing sitcoms with forbidden sex as the theme. Sex between relatives is a violation of the law with a penalty of imprisonment.

Gilda was not a virgin. She had pre-marital sex with her boyfriend who was her date at the prom. He deflowered her and soon she had dalliances with a host of other boys,. Jonas suggested to her that maybe she should get laid by a crew of construction workers. Maybe she needed a new surrounding to distract her mind from impure thoughts. One time, Larry and Jonas brought Gilda to a secluded island down south. The clear blue waters and the fresh breeze invigorated her mind that it staved off unwholesome innuendos for a while. It›s as if she looked at nature at it's finest. Before she went to the beach, she was irritable and ill-humored. Her temper would flare up at the slightest annoyance. You can see that the expression on her face was more tranquil now, showing signs of appeasement and submission. She wasn't the only girl in the family with multiple sex partners. Her two other sisters who were living abroad went out frequently with men but they were financially independent and solitary dwellers. She berated her boyfriend for not marrying her. She touseled his ebony hair resulting in a skirmish outside their home. She deplored the fact that she didn't have a husband and taunted her younger sister for not having one either. She would mumble on the phone that she would marry the scion of a rich family. She would recite a lot of possible candidates to be her lawfully wedded husband. A female cousin asked her how many men did she want. She was a fickle-minded lady who wanted men to follow her every whim. Inspite of her fervent desire to be loved, she was empty-handed. She had a whole wardrobe of dresses and would change ten times a day. She had an impressive jewelry collection which she inherited from a rich aunt but when hard times came, she was forced to pawn it to her sister. She had a nose that didn't look right because of a botched surgery. Whenever Jonas would drive the car to the mall, Manuel and Gilda would come along. Jonas would tell Gilda to sit at the back seat to avoid unnecessary sexual stimulation. You'll never know which hand will reach out to the spot between your legs. Jonas has seen the head of Gilda go up and down in her boyfriend's car. It were better that a brother be with other men because you're in the same line of thought. Many times the mind of Jonas was flooded with unclean thoughts. This was another reason why Jonas wanted to leave the family home.

Jonas passed the interview with a female consul at the Canadian embassy with flying colors. He impressed her with his high educational attainment showing his diploma and transcript of records, as well as, a cumulative work experience during his stint as a teacher at the university. He took a 747 jet with stop-overs at Tokyo and Detroit before landing in Montreal. He stayed in the apartment of two sisters, Terry and Lydia

Fuentes, before renting an apartment of his own. The province had just finished holding a referendum on independence which it narrowly lost. A lot of businesses relocated to nearby Toronto due to political uncertainty. Unity within the Canadian federation was a sensitive topic for francophones in Quebec as they badly wanted a country to call their own. They had their own language which thy wanted to nurture so that it grows and becomes the only official language in the affairs of the state, as well as, the language of commerce and diplomacy. Anyone who was going to do business in Quebec better do it in French so that they are better understood and avoid paying penalties. Jonas would put his French into practice by conversing with customers in a bakery. Soon he was taking orders for different kinds of bread like rye, onion or pumpernickel. He was also adept at the various flavors of muffins like bran, apple cinnamon or cranberry.

Sometimes he would work seven days a week due to lack of personnel. He developed a friendship with a Greek woman who was head of operations at the bakery. She drove a car and lived about an hour from downtown Montreal. She would sell Jonas jackets at a heavily discounted price. You had to protect yourself from the cold that sweeps through the province in the winter. He adjusted well to the different patterns in the weather. When he first saw snow, tears welled up in his eyes unable to contain his glee. The Greek lady would make rice pudding sprinkled with cinnamon and offer him a cup. She was a kind hearted woman, one who would go out of her way to help you. She had a son who had a drinking problem and was always asking her for money. They would get into scraming matches over the phone and she felt as if he were not her son. He eventually acceded to his mother's wishes and left the family house. Soon the Greek woman retired and Jonas was forced to look for another job.

The owner of the building where Jonas lived was a sympathetic man. He had an impressive coin collection from a wide array of countries and dating beck to antiquity. He'd been collecting coins since he was ten years old and was passionate about numismatics. He had a beautiful three story house on a one way street and antique dealers would visit his home to sell their wares.

When his brother died, he acquired the whole house for himself and placed his only daughter on the first floor. He could've had more children because he was going out with many women but due to a vasectomy done shortly after his daughter was born, he produced no more sperm. Jonas would do household chores for him. Fix his bed, go to the grocery to shop for food, and deposti money in the bank. He enjoyed the leisurely life in Canada and couldn't wait until he turned the age of 65. Seniors enjoyed a lof of benefits including a fifty per cent discount on their monthly bus passes and eligibility for a place at a government subsidized home. Jonas took advantage of the free visits to the doctor especially since he was diagnosed with diabetes and had to see a specialist to regulate his sugar level. His standard of living was a far cry from what he was used to in the Far East. You paid everytime you saw a doctor and with a poor respiratory condition, you had to shell out a hundred thousand pesos just to get a CT scan. On the other hand, in Canada, you get it for free. He never thought his instruction in French would turn out to be useful. He read French newspapers and watched French TV shows trying to grasp what they were saying. By now, due to the exposure, he could carry a conversation in French. There was a high concentration of blacks who complained of raical profiling. Jonas encountered instances of racism, but he learned to live with it and accept it as a part of life.

Elsa left early in the morning and headed to the police station to get an update on the search for the prime suspect in the murder case. Seated in a chair beside the desk of the chief of police, he broke the bad news to her. There were unverified reports that the suspect slipped out of the country posing as a foreign national. The description of the passenger matched the records on file although his conduct was calm and collected and could easily have fooled a most meticulous examination. He wore denim pants, rubber shoes and a white t-shirt with a Nike logo. He spoke heavily accented English and had difficulty understanding the questions. He could pass off as a tourist and had a camera dangling around his neck. He answered a routine set of questions and there was never any doubt in the officer's mind that he was a bona fide tourist. It was only after the ship set sail that they came to the conclusion that they made a mistake. Elsa was distraught at hearing this piece of news and deplored the apparent bungling of the case. The chief of police told Elsa that the destination of the suspect was somewhere in the Caribbean and that it was hard to force him to return home to face criminal charges. They surmised that probably he was in cahoots with a wealthy financier who paid for his trip. They had the passenger manifest which they carefully scrutinized for any leads that may bring them to the suspect's accomplice. Even with this information, there was no guarantee that they could trace the whereabouts of the suspect. Maybe if the designated country could review their list of inhabitants by carrying out a nationwide census, they would be able to locate and purge undocumented migrants. The alleged name on the suspect's passport was Tony Wingfield but this person was never reported to have arrived at the port of entry. The customs officer failed to coordinate with the record keeping division of the department of immigration to identify any spurious representation. The Bureau of Immigration promptly notified the government of the host country of the irregularity and they said they would look into it. Elsa prayed that the system of government was more efficient in other lands in the hopes of bringing back the suspect to face justice for his horrendous crime. Soon, Roger would be living off the fat of the land, taking pleasure in his newfound freedom albeit as a clandestine immigrant. Roger would be immune from prosecution because they could never determine his true identity. He blended well with the local population showing the same physical characteristics such as black eyes, wavy hair and swarthy complexion. Ultimately, Roger would have to fix his papers and acquire legal status to be able to stay in his new country. With the backing of his friend and mentor Philip Whitmore, he might very well be able to achieve that. As he surfaces out of his anonymity, then and only then will the authorities be able to pounce on him and book him on charges of murder. But this was thousands of miles away and it was hard to pinpoint Roger from among the teeming millions of people. Roger's future was secure and he didn't have to bother answering questions that could jeopardize his situation. He learned never to volunteer information just keep your secrets to yourself. He might supply knowledge of his existence that would incriminate him so it was better to keep mum on these issues.

But Elsa wouldn't take this sitting down. She urged the members of the constabulary to quit bickering and finding fault with one another and instead to put in more effort at finding the suspect. She urged the leader of the country to recall its ambassador and cut diplomatic ties until they catch the criminal. The foreign government was faced with a daunting task of rummaging through their records to see if there is any illegal alien living in their midst that matches the description of the suspect. There should be coordinated teamwork in the foreign country so they can hunt down the suspect wherever he may be.

The visit of Elsa to the police station was not at all pleasant. The chief of police told her not to poke her nose into their business. They were doing their job although it was met with many delays and interruption. Her intrusion into their affair would only muddle the investigation. They needed a name so they could search their records. A photo of the suspect wopuld help bolster the inquiry and they scanned the profiles of known criminals to see if there was a match. As it is, it was like looking for a pin in a haystack. The video of the suspect could not be relied upon because of the inferior quality of the footage. It's as if the case could never be solved with the suspect still on the lam and out of reach for law enforcement. She wasn't going to sit by and watch the felon go unpunished. She would go on brainstorming to come up with an idea. She would ask for a dialogue with the president to toughen anti-crime units and to tighten controls at departure gates even for foreigners. Attention from the highest office in the land was needed to stamp out crime. To modernize methods of trapping criminals from their hideout so that they can spend the rest of their time in jail. There can be no reprieve for people who commit heinous offences. It was one of the campaign promises of the president to fight crime and to guarantee a speedy trial. All measures should be taken so that there should be no miscarriage of justice and that all evidence presented should be carefully weighed and validated. Too many criminals are avoiding sentencing due to lax judicial procedures and loopholes in the system. One such example was an accused drug trafficker whose charges against him were dropped due to the slow pace of the trial. You can't keep a suspect in jail for more than sixty days unless charges are laid against him.

Elsa had had enough of the inefficiency of the police force charged in carrying out the investigation. She called a bunch of supporters to rally in front of the consulate of the Caribbean nation where Roger was reportedly hiding. Reporters and TV crews swarmed the place and got to interview Elsa about the steps she›ll take to have the suspect deported. An interview with the liaison officer of the consulate yielded a vague reaction saying the problem lied in this country›s internal affairs and how they handled the investigation. It could not be ascertained whether Roger was indeed in the Caribbean nation but their consulate issued a communique that they didn›t tolerate illegal immigrants expecially with a criminal background. Roger could be tried in absentia and if found guilty, the government could issue a shoot to kill order.

Wanted: dead or alive. As time passed, the chances of finding the culprit had become more and more remote. She slunk to her bed and raised her hands up in the air to signify that she had already given up. Just a naked body on the bed with his throat slashed and nobody to blame. Somebody must be held accountable for this gruesome murder. But it seems that the cuckoo bird had successfully flown away from the coop. It seems that there was no remedy for an inept police force who could not carry out an exhaustive search for a missing suspect.

Later in the day, Elsa got a visit from her Chinese friend, Sun-Ying who invited her to the Buddhist temple for some meditation exercises to relax her weary mind. They were squatting on the floor following the monotonous drone of a monk dressed in a gray robe and clean-shaven who was chanting some hymns on the microphone. Elsa could not understand what was being said because it was in a foreign language but went along bowing before several white statues of the Buddha. The succession of words in one unvaried key or pitch had a hypnotic effect that served to ease her tense muscles and soothe her mind. They lit incense and prayed for a quick resolution of the case. There were many life-size statues of an erect Buddha at the front lawn and these had a calming effect on the visitor. But still the death of William went unavenged and she sought to change that by dint of sheer grit.

The death of William wasn›t the main concern of Elsa›s life. She relented to the fact that the investigation take its due course and embrace the results come what may. She had other things in mind like seeing a surgeon to correct facial abnormalities. She was offended by what Linda Duvalier said that she turned off men due to her ghastly appearance. Many times at a party, she›d be standing alone in a corner with no one to talk to like a wallflower because men found her face repulsive. She had an in-depth discussion with the maxillofacial surgeon who said that her jaw jutted out too prominently. It needed realignment and a reduction in bone density. Her forehead too needed to be chiseled because it was protruding too heavily that made her look like an ape. A team of surgeons would be needed to perform the operation, as well as, an anesthesiologist who›d put her in a self-induced coma. She won›t be conscious upon the duration of the surgery and her blood pressure will be checked intermittently to verify that her vital signs are normal. If she was allergic to any drugs, she should notify the surgeon beforehand. Her skin would be perfectly preserved because there were no pockmarks or wrinkles that would necessitate the layering of a new epidermis. Skin grafts are only applied to people suffering from third degree burns. Elsa was nowhere near this situation so that lessened the difficulty of the operation.

The surgeon was a very experienced doctor having remodelled the faces of accident victims or people with congenital defects. There was to be a drastic change in the appearance of Elsa from being a denizen in the jungle to a city girl with all the right connections. She didn't want to attract suitors because romance was the farthest thing from her mind. She was beyond that. She just wanted to be appealing to the public in general so she can make many friends. She had no dreams of becoming a pin-up girl or pose for the cover of Vogue. She just wanted to be warmly received by her own coterie of friends maybe widen her sphere of influence by including people who were aloof to her. Many times during a ride in an elevator, she'd get sideswiped by people jostling for a place. Or in a crowded mall, to be sent at the back of the line to wait endlessly for her turn at the till. Now no more will people relegate her to the sidelines but will volunteer their places so she gets first in line. She would no longer be known as the bulldog of the borough of St. Leonard but the girl with the dainty black curls because of her penchant for using rollers on her hair before she retired to bed. The operation took four hours. After, the doctor went to the hospital room of Elsa with a hand-held mirror to show the marked improvement of her face. She looked at her reflection and straightaway she said she was pleased with the results. Her face was still a bit swollen, heavily bandaged because it was fresh from surgery. The sutures would be removed after the wounds heal and would reveal a whole new woman. She commissioned an artist to paint a portrait of herself stroking a cat and sitting in a pin-striped sofa. It turned out to be an accurate depiction of her facets striking a regal pose. She was happy and content with the favorable reaction of her friends. Her manners were more refined now underlining a feminine touch to all things that she carried out. Whereas before she would only wear pants and sit like a man, now she would wear skirts and cross her legs. She was enjoying being a girl again ever since her rude awakening into a world dominated by male chauvinist pigs. Men would often compliment her for the extraordinary way she looked. It was a far cry from the days when she was an ugly duckling and no one would even notice her. She won't be cooped up in her apartment anymore but go out with friends and meet new people. Elsa was a perfect example of a metamorphosis. A caterpillar spins a cocoon and a beautiful butterfly with bright colored wings emerges and flies to the pale blue sky. The new face of Elsa would open doors for her no doubt but it remains to be seen whether she can charm her way to the hearts of the people around her.